THE THING
IN THE BROOK

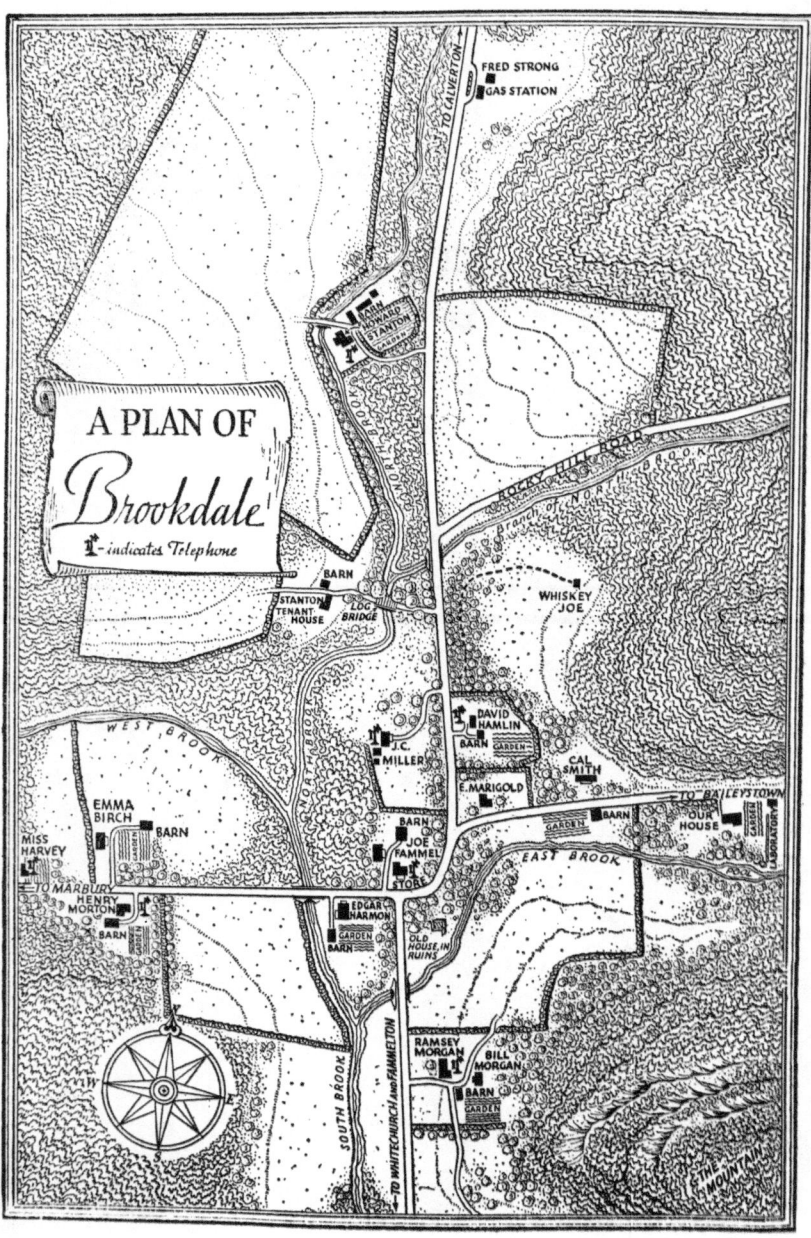

THE THING
IN THE BROOK

PETER STORME

COACHWHIP PUBLICATIONS
Greenville, Ohio

The characters (with the exception of Tinkel) and the situations in this book are wholly fictional and imaginative; do not portray, and are not intended to portray, any actual persons or parties.

The Thing in the Brook
© 2020 Coachwhip Publications

First published 1937
   Peter Storme, pseudonym
   Philip Van Doren Stern (1900-1984)
No claims made on public domain material.
Cover image: Noose © Amebar Studio

CoachwhipBooks.com

ISBN 1-61646-493-3
ISBN-13 978-1-61646-493-6

CHAPTER I
THE FRUIT OF THE SYCAMORE TREE

It was dark when I turned off the macadam to enter the dirt road that runs along the edge of the North Brook. It was only a short distance from home and I was feeling good. I had a car full of fine specimens that I had collected up-state. There was enough material to keep me busy at the microscope for days and I was happily whistling "A Capital Ship for an Ocean Trip" as I spun Little Bertha swiftly along the narrow shelflike road. It is dangerous for a stranger to drive on that road at night, for it goes steadily downhill and winds and curves through dense woods, but I knew every foot of the way and was even getting some slight pleasure from making Bertha scamper around the turns. I knew I could spot the lights of an oncoming car long before I came close to it, so I was making even better time than I would in daylight.

Suddenly I saw a man with a dimly lit lantern right in the middle of the road. I shoved Bertha over quickly; she bumped over some loose stones on the inner edge of the road, and then plunged into a soft bank of dirt with a quivering sigh. The lights went out and the engine stopped abruptly. I untangled myself from the wheel, and wiggled out of my hat which had been pushed down over my eyes. The man came running up swinging his lantern.

It was George Hathaway who worked on Howard Stanton's farm.

"You hurt?" he asked.

"No," I said, "but what's the idea of walking in the middle of the road like that?"

"You shouldn't drive so fast," he answered mildly. "Your car smashed?"

"I don't know. Wait till I get a light so I can look at her."

I dug my flashlight out of the door pocket while he puttered uselessly around the front of the car with his miserable lantern.

"She don't seem hurt," he said, "'cept for the mudguard."

I threw the bright rays of my flashlight over the front end of Bertha.

"Ain't even blowed the tire," he observed cheerfully.

"Do you suppose you can pull that fender back into shape?" I asked.

He put his lantern down carefully, took a firm hold on the fender and tugged. The flimsy sheet metal bent easily under his powerful hands—too easily, in fact, for it came back too far. Patiently he pushed it down a little.

"See if the engine'll start up," he said. "I'll stay here and shove."

I crawled into the car and found that the sudden jar had thrown my leg against the switch and shut the engine off. I turned the switch back and stepped on the starter. In a moment the engine was running with the sweet purr that is characteristic of Bertha when she is at her best. I turned the lights on and backed her out on the road without any trouble.

"She's all right," I said. "Want a lift?"

"No. I'm just going down the road a piece to look for Howard. He stayed in the hayfield at the tenant farm and he ain't showed up yet. Howard wouldn't want to let the last scrap of hay get away from him."

"Well, jump on the running board," I said, "and I'll help you look. You won't see much with that lantern."

"That's a real Stanton lantern," he chuckled. "Twenty years old and wasn't no good when it was new."

It was only a few hundred feet to the break in the woods that marked the entrance to the Stanton tenant farm. We left the car on the side of the road.

I knew George Hathaway fairly well. I had often gone rabbit hunting with him. He is a good rabbit hunter because he has the type of mentality that permits him to put himself in the place of a rabbit and guess what it will do next.

"How are the rabbits running this year?" I asked, in order to make conversation. "I haven't seen many. It looks as if the hunting would be poor as usual."

"Oh, there's plenty of 'em. Trouble is the state keeps putting in them doggone Missouri rabbits and they don't play fair. They pop down a woodchuck hole or dive under a stone row before you can get near 'em. What we need is some good old-fashioned native rabbits like we used to have. I don't hold with bringing in them foreign rabbits. You better go ahead. I can't see the front of my own hat with this danged lantern."

To this day I can't explain why I had volunteered to help look for Howard Stanton. My acquaintance with the man was very slight and the little I had heard about him was hardly likely to make me want to know him any better. Most of the people in Brookdale were a pretty decent lot, but Stanton had the reputation of being a decidedly unpleasant person who could at the slightest provocation become downright nasty. He spent his spare time making sure that the "No Trespassing" signs on his four-hundred-acre farm were in perfect order, and he was always involved in petty lawsuits. According to local gossip, he had hounded his wife to death by his harsh treatment. He had had a housekeeper ever since she died. Only a good-natured but spineless fool like George Hathaway would work for him as farm hand, and I knew that Stanton drove him like a mule.

I would never even have ventured to set foot on his tenant farm if I hadn't been with George. As it was I had an uncomfortable feeling that the old man might be lurking behind a bush ready to spring out and raise merry hell with me for being there.

The driveway leading in to the farm plunges abruptly downward for a few feet and then runs through some brush before it reaches the brook. Wisps of hay were still hanging from the bushes where the wagon had brushed against them. There were scattered stones underfoot, so I proceeded slowly, keeping my light close to the ground. It was very dark under the huge sycamore trees that line the shore of the brook. I could see a crude log bridge there. I felt vaguely uneasy and stopped to let Hathaway catch up to me.

"He's probably not here," I said. "Why should he want to stay out in the dark?"

"He had a bottle of applejack with him," Hathaway said. "He may be dead drunk. It wouldn't be the first time I've had to drag his old carcass home in the middle of the night. Watch your step on that bridge. It's kind of rickety."

I went ahead cautiously, casting the light down on my feet. Suddenly I heard a low growl come from the darkness. I heard a scuffling sound on the other side of the brook. Then something rushed across the bridge at us. I stepped back hastily. A gaunt-looking police dog ran into the circle of light.

"It's all right," said Hathaway. "It's only Dempsey. Howard must be somewheres around. It's his dog."

He patted the huge animal's head.

"Where is he, Dempsey? Where's the boss?"

The dog growled in a low tone and licked Hathaway's hand.

"Where's the boss?" he repeated. "Come on, boy, show us where he is."

Dempsey turned and trotted across the bridge. I followed, watching my footing carefully on the uneven surface of rough logs. Hathaway waited on the shore.

"Come on," I said. "Hurry up or we'll lose sight of him."

The dog had gone ahead and was already beyond the narrow circle of light that my flashlight made. Suddenly I heard him howl dismally.

I stopped short as I felt something touch my face. I started and it slid away. Then it swung back again and touched me lightly on the cheek. I stepped back quickly, almost losing my balance. Hathaway had come up close behind me and put out a steadying hand.

"What's the matter?" he whispered.

I stood there absolutely frozen for a moment. Hathaway began to shake my arm.

"Something hit me in the face," I said finally. I fumbled with the flashlight nervously so that I almost dropped it into the water. Then I cast its rays upwards. There was a long gray shape suspended from a tree limb and hanging over the bridge. I suddenly realized what it was. I threw the light up higher. There was a white face above it; its eyes and tongue protruded horribly, and as the body turned slowly around, I could see that the back of the head was smashed in. There was blood all over everything.

CHAPTER II
ENTER THE POLICE

I suppose everyone has wondered what he would do if he suddenly came upon the corpse of a murdered man. I had seen plenty of stiffs when I was studying anatomy at college so they were no novelty to me, but I'll confess that when I was confronted with the freshly murdered body of Howard Stanton I acted as childishly afraid as though I had never seen a dead man before. Still, I must say that there is a lot of difference between seeing a properly prepared cadaver neatly laid out on a slab and bumping into a gory corpse in the middle of the night. I was still somewhat quivery as I backed off the bridge to get a foothold on the solid earth again.

"Golly, he's dead all right," I said to Hathaway just so I could hear the sound of my own voice. "The whole back of his head is smashed."

"Think we ought to cut him down?"

"What for? He's dead. We'd better let the police see him just as he is. They might raise an awful howl if we touch the body. Come on, let's go and phone them."

We hurried back to the car. Hathaway pulled out a package of tobacco and bit off a huge quid. I stuffed my pipe and lit it. I had trouble holding the match steadily.

"Well?" I asked impatiently.

Hathaway said nothing. I could hear him munching his vile chewing tobacco.

"Look here," I said to Hathaway suddenly, "I don't see why this should be any affair of mine. Suppose I take you to a phone so you can call the police. Tell them you found the body. Leave me out of it. I've got a lot of work to do and I can't afford to get tangled up in an affair like this anyway." I had a book to finish and I had only six weeks in which to do it.

"No sir," he said with sudden shrewdness. "If I tell the cops I found the body they may try to hang the murder on me. You're my witness."

I sat there cursing myself for having offered to help him look for Stanton. I could have been home safely out of all this.

"How do I know you didn't do it?" I asked bluntly.

"Well, you don't suppose I'd have been fool enough to take you down there to see the body if I had, do you?"

The thought crept into my mind that it might have been a very smart way for a murderer to act in order to build up an alibi. Still I had offered to help him without his asking me and anyway a bright idea like that was certainly beyond Hathaway's mediocre intellect.

"I guess I'm in for it," I said wearily. "Let's get to a telephone."

"We got a phone in the house. We can go there."

I turned the car around and drove to the Stanton farmhouse. There was a light burning in the kitchen. I shall never forget the sudden strange cry that Mrs. Denner, Stanton's housekeeper, uttered when Hathaway told her that her employer was dead. After this one burst of emotion she became grimly silent and sat stiff and straight on her chair without looking at either of us.

I called the local state police headquarters at Fammelton. It would take them about half an hour to make the run, even at top speed. We sat down to wait. There was no way I could get in touch with my wife. We had no telephone in our house. I didn't like leaving her alone but I had no choice in the matter.

Hathaway's face was drawn. His clumsy fingers picked jerkily at the brim of his battered straw hat as he told me what had happened before I met him on the road. Stanton had stayed in the field to clean up the scattered bits of ungathered hay and had sent Hathaway to take the wagon back to the barn. It had been almost dark when he left the tenant farm. When night fell, Mrs. Denner began to worry and had asked him to take the lantern and look for his employer.

"Did Mr. Stanton have any enemies?" I asked.

"Well, I guess he did," he said, looking cautiously at Mrs. Denner. "He was kind of short-tempered, you know."

"Any particular enemies?"

"Mr. Stanton was a wealthy man," Mrs. Denner said unexpectedly. "There were many people who envied his success. You can't get money without treading on somebody's toes."

I wondered why she had been so terribly affected by the announcement of Stanton's death. It was rumored that she had been his mistress. She wasn't bad-looking, about thirty-four or so, and slightly plumpish. Her skin was unusually white for a person who lived in the country and her hands seemed to be soft and well cared for. She had large black eyes, rather pretty ones, but her mouth was thin and tight.

"Is there anyone you suspect, Mrs. Denner?" I asked.

She gave me a curious stare, shook her head, and said nothing.

I leaned back in my chair and looked around the kitchen. Farmhouse kitchens, generally speaking, are pleasant enough in the daytime, but at night in the feeble glow of a single kerosene lamp they have a morguelike quality that makes everyone look haggard and sinister. Stanton's kitchen was furnished in the customary mail-order style. He may have been a wealthy man but the water in his house was supplied by an iron pump in a wood-encased sink. It has always been a source of wonder to me why so many farmers will spend considerable sums of money to house their cattle in luxury while they themselves are perfectly contented to live like squatters.

Hathaway's big honest face was troubled. He kept twisting his straw hat in his hands until the brim tore. Then he placed it carefully on the table.

"Do you think they're likely to make trouble for me?" he asked gloomily.

I tried to think of a reassuring answer. Just then we heard the faint sound of a police siren coming through the distant hills. Hathaway looked around apprehensively and went to the window to peer out.

A few moments later the police descended upon us. They came in as if they had expected to besiege the house and I found myself the center of their inquiry.

"—hanging from a tree . . . his head bashed in. Yes, not far from here," I was saying, among a great many other things. And then we left the house and started in the big police car toward the tenant farm. Mrs. Denner had mercifully been left behind.

I gathered that the man beside me was the captain. At any rate he had a gold badge while the other men wore silver ones. He also had an extraordinarily red face and a thick neck.

"I have nothing to do with this," I told him. "I'm just a neighbor. I happened to pick up Stanton's farm hand on the road and I was with him when the body was found."

They all piled out with big searchlights. Stanton's dog greeted us with an unpleasant growl. The body was hanging quite still now. I noticed for the first time that there was a pool of blood on the bridge.

"Nice job," the captain grunted. "When you get a murder back here in the sticks it's usually a pretty good one."

We stared for a moment at the motionless corpse. One of the men went toward it.

"Better let it stay there, boys," he called out. "The coroner's on his way up."

He walked back to the road and motioned to me and Hathaway to accompany him. His heavy body lumbered up the slope and he stumbled on the stony path, cursing as he went.

"Well?" I said. "What now?"

"Tell it to me all over again," he said, "and tell it slow."

In great detail I went over the whole story once more. The captain said nothing. Suddenly he turned to Hathaway and asked him what he had to say. The poor fellow was almost incoherent, and I couldn't help thinking that he would surely have been held for the murder if my story had not corroborated his.

Another car drew up. It contained the coroner, a doctor, and a police photographer. The captain placed us in the charge of a lanky trooper who placidly started to chew gum as soon as his superior officer left us to go back to the scene at the brook.

"They're not going to take me down to police headquarters tonight, are they?" I asked the trooper anxiously. "My wife's waiting for me."

"That's up to Captain Macready," he said, "He's going to want to ask you a lot more questions anyway."

They took us back to the Stanton house and drew up the kitchen table as though they were going to hold a court of inquiry. One of the troopers sat down with a pad while the captain took off his cap and mopped his brow with a handkerchief. He had grayish hair, short-cropped and stubby. There was a scar across the top of the forehead, running into the hair. He began to fire questions at me.

"Name?"

"James Whitby."

"Residence?"

"Here—Brookdale, that is. I live on the road to Bailey-stown."

"Mm. How long have you lived here?"

"About five years."

"Business?"

"I'm an assistant professor of biology at the State College."

"Any identification?"

I produced my driver's license and a college card.

"Did you know this guy Stanton?"

"Very slightly."

"Know anything about him?"

"Not very much. He wasn't very popular, but if he had any real enemies I don't know who they are."

And then he made me go over the story of finding the body all over again. I was growing heartily sick of the whole business.

"All right, that's all," the captain said at last and beckoned to Hathaway to come to the table.

"How about letting me go home now?" I asked. "I've told you my story three times. It must be getting rather dull."

He looked up with annoyance. "Home? Well, yes, I guess so. We can get you there when we need you?"

"Any time at all. I'm supposed to be on a vacation."

"Okay. Run along then, Professor."

I hurried out without paying any attention to George Hathaway's despairing glances. I wanted to get away from that fantastic nightmare as quickly as I could.

I knew that Joan had expected me to be home by dark and that she must have been waiting for hours. It was past midnight now. She had our dachshund Tinkel for company, but Tinkel is no protection because she is such a friendly little beast that she would undoubtedly welcome an intruder as a new playmate. I was worried but I resolved to take the situation firmly in hand before Joan could get in a word of reproach. I sounded Bertha's anemic horn as I came up the road to our house and I was relieved to see Joan step out holding Tinkers wriggling little body.

"Now don't make noises," I said snapping off the headlights. "I'm terribly late and I know it, but when you hear what happened. . . ."

"I know, you had three flat tires and were captured by Indians."

"I've been held by the police," I said impressively. "I was practically arrested but I talked them into letting me go. I'm the star witness in a murder case. I found Howard Stanton's body hanging from a tree."

Joan stared at me solemnly for a moment. Then she said: "You'd better think up a better excuse."

"Damn it, I don't need any excuse. The police have been questioning me for hours. I'm worn out. I tell you, I . . ."

"Did they use the third degree on you?"

"No, they didn't," I said sweetly. "They probably realized that I am so used to third-degree methods at home that such things wouldn't have any effect on me." I went into the house and locked myself in the bathroom.

I was vigorously brushing my teeth when I heard a gentle tap on the door. I paid no attention.

Joan rattled the door knob. "May I come in?" she asked in a doleful voice. "It's awfully lonesome out here and I'm scared."

I opened the door and put my arms around her. Tinkel slid in through the half-opened door and sat down to watch us gravely.

"I'm sorry," I said through the toothpaste. "But you should have believed me. I really did find Stanton's body and the police did hold me."

"I know," she said. "But has it occurred to you that if you did, then I've been all alone for hours with a murderer roaming around?"

"Yes, it has, but you didn't know there was a murderer."

"But I know it now."

"So that made you afraid all evening?"

She nodded. "I'm awfully glad you're back. Tell me what happened."

This was about the fourth time I had to tell the story of finding Stanton's body, so I was able to make a good tale out of it for Joan. It was after one o'clock when I finished.

"You'd better take the dog for a walk now," Joan said.

"It won't do any good. She never knows what it's for," I protested.

"You're afraid to go out."

"Don't be absurd," I said. "I'm tired and I know it's useless."

"Come on, I'll go out with you."

We took the flashlight and went out on the road together. Tinkel ran along sniffing happily every few feet, but I was right. Nothing happened.

CHAPTER III
LOCAL HISTORIAN EXTRAORDINARY

I suppose I should have had trouble falling asleep that night but I didn't. I did dream, but what it was about I don't remember. When I awoke the sunshine was pouring into the room and everything that had happened the night before seemed very far away.

Joan was already awake. Her long red hair was spread out on the pillow around her and she was staring idly out of the window. She turned around to greet me with a good morning grin.

"We ought to invite Henry Hale out for the weekend," she said, apropos of nothing.

"Why should we?"

"Because he'd love it. You know what a murder mystery fan he is."

"This isn't a murder mystery. It's a murder. The real thing—not some writer's wild imagination, Henry would be an awful nuisance. He'd be under the feet of the police all the time."

"I think we ought to invite him anyway."

"Okay. Then we'll invite him. I suppose we have to invite someone for the weekend. We always do. It might as well be Henry. This whole business is going to ruin my working schedule anyway."

I got up and looked out the window across the wide valley to the mountain that serves as our backyard. It was a glorious day. The dew was still sparkling on the grass and the brook glistened, in the clear morning sunlight.

"Shall we start the day with a dip in the brook?" I asked.

Joan hesitated a minute and then grabbed her bathrobe. "All right. Last one in makes breakfast!"

We dashed through the kitchen, carefully avoiding |Tinkel's copy of yesterday's *Times,* and raced down to the little tree-lined swimming pool in the back of the house. Tinkel ran with us, barking frantically.

Joan played a typically feminine trick. She had only thrown her robe around her shoulders. She dropped it on the grass and jumped into the water with her nightgown on and then leisurely proceeded to take off the dripping garment while I was still struggling to get out of my pajamas.

"I'll have a double portion of orange juice, dear. And see that you don't burn the toast," she said calmly.

"There is something inherently deceitful about women," I said as I slowly took off my clothes, "some innate weakness in their characters that makes them always try to gain their ends by unfair means. They are conceived through the guile of their mothers; as little girls they have winning ways that make the forthright honesty of little boys seem crude and boorish; and then as they grow up they come into the possession of their mothers' original guile and so start the vicious circle all over again. They are notoriously poor sportsmen. They don't believe in hunting, but they can never understand why you don't shoot a sitting bird. They loathe prize fighting but they. . . ."

"Did you come down here to bathe or to deliver a lecture on why women are smarter than men?" Joan interrupted rudely. "If you're going to orate I'd recommend that you put your clothes on and not stand there like that in full view of the road."

"All right, I'll make breakfast. But you clean up the kitchen first."

She made a face and plunged into the water again.

It was an excellent breakfast, and for a change the coffee was good. Women have no feeling for coffee. They don't approach it with the proper ceremony and they can never understand that it has to be prepared with scientific exactness just as if it were a laboratory culture.

Our house is an extraordinarily cheerful one on a sunny morning. The woodwork is painted white and most of the furniture is light-colored maple or pine that we have picked up in the neighborhood. Joan complains that the treatises and reports on biological subjects that I have crammed into our shelves are not really books. But the framed flower prints and the huge Audubon bird plates are indisputably pictures—and very colorful ones, too.

We sat around the breakfast table, smoking after-coffee cigarettes. Joan was talking about Howard Stanton whom she had known much better than I had since she makes an effort to get around among our neighbors.

"I wonder if they'll have an auction sale now?" she mused. "I'll bet there's a lot of swell patchwork quilts in that house."

"Whether they have a sale depends on the heir, I guess. Who do you suppose it is?"

"Howard's brother, probably. The doctor."

"The one from Baileystown?"

"Mm. He wouldn't want patchwork quilts, would he? He's a bachelor."

"Don't be such a little ghoul," I said. "I believe you'd murder someone for a good patchwork quilt."

"Well, maybe someone like Howard Stanton," she admitted. "I'm sure he'll not be missed!"

"Except by the police. They seem quite perturbed."

"You don't think that housekeeper could have done it?" she demanded suddenly. "I never did like that woman. She has a sly look about her."

I explained patiently that it would have been utterly impossible for Mrs. Denner to have committed the murder. She had been in the house with Hathaway until he went out to look for Stanton. There just wasn't time enough for her to have done it.

I got up to go to the village to get Emma, our maid of all work.

"Well, then, perhaps she got George Hathaway to do it," Joan persisted. "Maybe he's in love with her. Maybe they wanted to get rid of Stanton. . . ."

"Save it for Henry," I told her. "He's going to be a lot more interested in this confounded murder than I am."

I headed the car toward the village. I was becoming more and more resentful of the way the Stanton murder case threatened to interfere with my work. I had spent more than a year on a book on the Myxomycetes of our state and my sabbatical leave would be up at the end of the summer. Joan was making the drawings for the book and we were both looking forward to its publication, since it would probably bring me promotion to a full professorship and a decent salary.

I was in desperate need of time but now there would probably be some sort of inquest, and I could foresee that the weekend with Henry would have to be given over to a pointless discussion of murder. Murder seems to me to have been given an exaggerated importance in modern life. After all, the extinction of one individual matters very little in any biological consideration of a species. I couldn't help wishing that Howard Stanton had picked out some other part of the country in which to get killed.

There was a state trooper in town when I drove through. His motorcycle was parked in front of Fammel's store while he was questioning a group of townspeople. The presence of such a person in a little place like Brookdale, of course, is an event of prime importance, comparable only to the erection of barricades in Times Square. The village was seething with excitement. Several people shouted to me as I passed, but I went grimly on.

Emma's house lies at the other end of the village. It is a small gray bungalow surrounded by rose bushes, lilacs, and small animals. Emma lives there alone but she has several cats, a hound dog, a vicious gander, and a flock of chickens to keep her company. She does our housework, but she can in no sense of the word be considered as a servant.

She is a woman of indeterminate age—anywhere between forty-five and sixty—and she is inordinately proud of her personal appearance. She was, I suppose, a good-looking woman when she was younger. She still spends a great portion of her tiny income trying to make herself alluring.

Hats and gloves are her greatest weaknesses. She always puts on a hat for the five-minute journey between her house and ours—and Emma's hat is something to put on! It has pins and things and takes time to adjust. But no matter how much time she spends trying, she never seems to get her hat on quite right—it is always either perched on the top of her head or jammed down over the bridge of her nose. Last winter Joan gave her a pair of knitted woolen gloves with each finger made of yarn of a different and hideously brilliant color. She was so proud of them that she kept right on wearing them all summer long.

When she first came to work for us, Emma had evidently never seen the kind of clothes the modern city-bred girl wears. She was tremendously impressed with Joan's silk underwear and the gossamer lightness of her stockings. "I suppose," she said in an awed voice, "you need things like those in your business."

Joan tells me that Emma has learned a great deal since then. She says that she even wears a corset now, although I haven't noticed that it makes any difference in her figure—but then I don't see how it could. She is a woman of very generous proportions and is large all over rather than in any one place.

She was sitting on the front porch waiting eagerly for me. A large bouquet of flowers for Joan was clutched firmly in her left hand and she had a number of mysterious paper parcels held tightly against her breast. She got into the car with some difficulty, making strange little chirping noises as she did so. Emma is the soul of good nature but she likes to talk and I was in no mood for a cross-examination. Since she gets up at five o'clock every morning she had had plenty of time to hear all about Howard Stanton's murder.

"Oh, Mr. Whitby," she began effusively, "isn't it just too terrible? And to think that you were the one to find him! What did he look like? Is it true that he? . . ."

"Emma," I said wearily, "I've had comparatively little sleep. I have a great deal of work to do. I never felt less like discussing the details of a murder case than I do right now. It's true that I was present when Howard Stanton's body was found last night. I'm very sorry that I was. But all I did was be there. I know nothing at all about the case. I don't even know how the man met his death. Now I'm sure that you must know more about it than I do, so why don't you tell me?"

She looked at me with amazement.

"But you found him," she protested. "You don't mean to say that you're not even going to tell me how he looked?"

"He looked terrible," I said briefly. "There was lots of blood—if that's what you want."

"Well, I do declare," she said sitting back in her seat, "if you aren't the funniest man."

We drove along the dusty road in silence—a difficult task for Emma. The trooper was still in front of the store and the crowd around him had grown larger. There aren't more than about seventy actual residents in Brookdale and its neighboring farms, but the news was evidently being spread by telephone, and automobiles were bringing curiosity seekers from points farther away.

"Aren't you going to stop?" Emma said, aghast at my evident intention to keep right on going.

"I certainly am not," I said stepping viciously on the accelerator. In another minute I had left the village behind and was urging Little Bertha up the gentle slope that leads to our house.

Emma made a small snuffling sound which I knew was the prelude to another disclosure.

"Did you know," she said, "that Howard had been choked to death?"

"No, I didn't," I said, startled out of my somnolence. "I saw his head all smashed."

Emma was delighted. "Well, he was choked first. Then they smashed his head with a rock. And then they took a rope from a tarpaulin in the hayfield and put it around his neck and hoisted him up in a tree."

"I don't suppose the police have found out who killed him, have they?"

"They don't seem to, because there was a trooper around asking everybody questions. I told him all about Howard and how mean he was."

"So now you've got yourself into it?"

"Well, he did take my name and he said he'd be around to ask me some more questions," she said proudly.

"You'd better watch out or they'll be suspecting that you did it."

Emma tittered nervously in a high-pitched voice that always irritated me. "Now, Mr. Whitby, you can't really mean that. Why, I never had anything against poor Howard."

"I thought you once told me that he threatened to have you arrested for trespassing when he caught you picking berries in his fields? Did you by any chance tell the trooper about that?"

"No, I didn't," she said, looking at me apprehensively. She was then silent for nearly a minute and I decided that perhaps I was being a little cruel.

"What else did you find out about that murder?" I asked.

"Well," she said shifting about eagerly, "it seems that most everybody in the village knew Howard was going to work late to get the hay in last night. Mrs. Denner called her cousin on the phone yesterday and she happened to mention it to her. Anybody could have listened in, of course."

"Did they?"

"It was Mrs. Morton who told me, and I don't know how she'd know unless she had—"

Emma paused significantly.

I nodded. "That settles it. Mrs. Morton killed him!" Mrs. Morton was an aggressively active member of the W.C.T.U. who had once called at our house to try to persuade me to sign a pledge.

Emma giggled. "You do say such things."

"By the way," I asked suddenly, "how many phones are there on that party line?"

"Why, nearly the whole village is on it! Let's see now, there's the Mortons, Howard Stanton, Fammel's store, the Hamlins, J. C. Miller, Ramsey Morgan, and Miss Harvey."

"I guess we can eliminate Miss Harvey."

Miss Harvey was an elderly spinster well past seventy who lived alone in a small stone house near Emma.

Joan had been puttering in the garden but she ran out to greet us, making appropriate murmurs of appreciation for Emma's flowers.

"I've got a little present for you," she said grinning at me and holding out a piece of white paper of legal appearance. "A state trooper just brought it here."

It was some kind of notice requesting me to be present at an inquest to be held on Thursday at two o'clock for the purpose of investigating the murder of Howard Stanton. I shoved it into my pocket with a grunt and went into the house to get some stationery so I could write to Henry. Joan followed Emma into the kitchen and the two of them immediately plunged into a detailed discussion of the crime.

I sat down in one of the deck chairs on the porch to write my letter. I could hear Emma telling Joan about the unpleasantness she had had with Howard Stanton over the berry-picking. She was slopping water over the breakfast dishes—she hated to wash dishes and was always delighted when someone would talk to her so she could take her mind off the disagreeable work.

I was certain that Henry would want to come out for the weekend. Henry is a mystery fan who has read, I suspect, more murder stories than any man alive. He is a walking encyclopedia on the subject although he had never had an opportunity to come in intimate contact with an actual murder case. In my letter I began to outline the details of the Stanton affair. As I wrote, I listened idly to the conversation going on inside the house. Then I decided that it might be a good idea to try to get some more information from Emma for Henry's benefit. I laid down my pen and went into the kitchen.

"Has there ever been a murder around here before?" I asked abruptly.

She looked startled, "No, I wouldn't exactly say there was—at least you couldn't call it a murder, because they never found out who had been killed, but we did have a sort of murder about twenty years ago. No, it must be nearer twenty-five."

"Well, what was it?" I demanded.

"It happened right near here, on the East Brook. Lyman Apgar was trout fishing and he found a girl's clothes, all piled up in a heap in the bushes. Even—" she lowered her voice—"even her underclothes. They searched the brook and the woods and up on the mountain but they never found her. They advertised in *The Rocket* but they never even found out who she was. It stands to reason that a girl wouldn't take off all her clothes and go wandering around—" she stopped abruptly, brought up short by the word "naked" which she was evidently about to use, gulped, and finished lamely—"without any clothes."

"Maybe she was in swimming when he came along and scared her away before she could get her clothes," Joan suggested.

"How could she get home without any clothes?"

"She might have waited till dark."

"She might have, but this happened early in the spring when it's still pretty cold. Anyway we don't have any girls around here who would go swimming like that. Without any clothes!"

Joan looked at me guiltily. I grinned and decided that we had better change the subject.

"Well, it doesn't seem to have much connection with this case," I said. "Tell me, who do you think killed Howard Stanton?"

"I don't like to think it was anyone from around here," Emma said. "Maybe it was a tramp. There's lots of tramps who might have done it."

"That's nonsense, Emma, and you know it. Did you ever see a tramp on these back roads?"

She admitted that she never had. Brookdale was ten miles from a railroad or a main highway and no tramp in his right senses would venture into such sparsely settled country.

"Did you find out whether the body had been robbed?"

"It hadn't," she answered briefly. "His gold watch was there and nearly a hundred dollars."

"I guess that finishes your tramp theory."

"I can't believe that anybody around here would do it though," she repeated.

I tried another tack.

"Was there anything in Stanton's past life that might furnish a reason for the murder?"

"I couldn't say right off that there was anything," Emma began slowly. "Of course he did have a fight at one time or another with almost everybody around here. He hasn't been on speaking terms with J. C. Miller for more than ten years now on account of some argument they had over boundaries. He got mad at Joe Fammel and never goes—I meant, went—to the store. He always sent George Hathaway down instead. He even had a fight with Mrs. Morton because she wanted him to sign a temperance pledge, and then he threatened to have the law on Whiskey Joe because he found him lying drunk in the ditch along the road by his farm entrance. He said it was trespassing. He was a holy terror against trespassers. What was his was his and he wouldn't allow anybody an inch. He was always very uncongealed."

Joan glanced quickly at me. I avoided her eyes. This was no time for improving Emma's English.

"He must have been pretty well off, wasn't he?" I asked.

"Oh, sure he was," she answered. "He had lots of money. He'd spend it right enough buying a thoroughbred bull or a new tractor but he'd never spend a penny on himself. I don't suppose he's bought a hat since he was a young man."

"Was he always like that?" Joan asked.

"No, he wasn't. I've heard that he led a very fast life when he was in the army."

"In the army?—"

"Yes, he volunteered in the Spanish-American War. A lot of our boys did. Howard was in Cuba with Teddy Roosevelt, but after he came back and got married and settled down on his father's farm he didn't even want to talk about his army days. Most of the other boys were pretty proud of being in the war, but Howard always said that it was just foolishness, which, in a way, I suppose it was," Emma said reflectively.

The dishes were finished now and Emma was ready to begin her daily task of cleaning the house. I had only one more question to ask.

"Do you know who will be the heir to Stanton's money?"

"His brother, Dr. Allen Stanton," she replied promptly. "And a good man he is, too. As different from Howard as can be. At least I suppose he'll be the heir. It would be just like Howard to will his money to a cat and dog home so he could spite his brother."

"Was there any bad feeling between them?"

"No, not that I know of. But Howard didn't exactly have good feeling toward anyone—except himself."

I left Emma in peace to do her cleaning, which she disliked even more than washing dishes. Cooking was her art and she displayed for her other duties the disdain which every true creator has for the annoying details of life that take time away from the practice of his chosen art.

Joan came out on the porch with me. I hurriedly finished the letter to Henry, summarizing what Emma had confided to me, and told him that I would expect him Friday evening on the 7:27 train. He had plenty of time to let me know whether or not he could make it, for this was only Wednesday morning. I attached a special delivery stamp to the envelope.

That was a mistake.

CHAPTER IV
INTRODUCING HENRY

I discovered that it was a mistake when I was awakened the next morning at an unreasonably early hour by the sound of someone knocking at our kitchen door. Tinkel was barking shrilly.

Joan opened one eye and looked at me expectantly.

"You go," she said sleepily. "It's probably the murderer."

I got out of bed and went downstairs. Tinkel greeted me with enthusiasm and then made a bolt for the stairs. I could hear Joan shriek as the dog jumped on the bed to lick her face.

There was a small boy with a bicycle waiting for me. He thrust a yellow envelope into my hand.

"Telegram," he said unnecessarily and then demanded a dollar for delivering it.

The ten-mile trip was certainly worth it, but I always curse my precipitate friends who send me telegrams instead of letting their usually unimportant messages be delivered a few hours later by the regular rural free delivery, I tore open the envelope and read:

ARRIVE WHITECHURCH THIS MORN-
ING EIGHT SIXTEEN DAYLIGHT STOP
WILL YOU MEET TRAIN STOP HOPE YOU
WONT MIND WILL EXPLAIN LATER
                                    HENRY

It was almost 7:30. It would take me half an hour to get to Whitechurch over our dirt roads.

I went upstairs and showed Joan the telegram. She looked at it drowsily and snuggled back into her pillow muttering uncomplimentary things about Henry. She promptly fell asleep again while I dressed hurriedly.

Tinkel had burrowed under the covers of Joan's bed and was sleeping happily. I hauled her out unceremoniously by the scruff of the neck and took her downstairs with me. The kitchen floor, as usual, had to be attended to.

I drove down to the station, musing bitterly on the manner in which my quiet existence had been disturbed. I had managed to get some work done on my book during the previous afternoon and evening, even though several people from the village had dropped in on visits that were ostensibly social. Fortunately, Joan and I had been shut up in the laboratory when they arrived and Emma had gotten rid of them. But now I was to have Henry Hale on my hands—and two days sooner than I had expected him.

Henry works in what I have always considered the most prosaic business in the world—cotton converting. I don't know much about cotton converting but it seems fearfully dull to me, and the cotton section around Worth Street looks like a hangover from the dreariest days of nineteenth century mercantilism. It is my firm belief that Henry's inordinate passion for murder is a natural reaction from the uninteresting nature of his daily occupation.

I have known Henry ever since we were freshmen at the state college where I now teach. His mind is of the super-ficial type that interests itself in many subjects without mastering any one of them. In college he had apparently never spent any time studying, yet he always managed to get fairly good marks, and he had finally been awarded a Phi Beta Kappa key. He promptly lost it, of course. Henry always loses things that embarrass him.

He has many peculiarities. He loves to boast about the qualities that he doesn't possess but he is very shy when anyone praises him for the few good ones he actually does have. He is very generous but he loathes being thanked for anything. He is extraordinarily considerate of old ladies, small children and simple people of any kind but he hates to be looked upon as being in any way sentimental. As a result, he tries, rather pathetically sometimes, to appear hard-boiled.

In appearance he is strikingly undistinguished. He is quick and wiry, of medium height and he is most certainly not at all the swaggering extrovert that he makes himself out to be. Henry loves to shock people by telling them outrageous stories when he first meets them and he delights in puncturing inflated egos. He has absolutely no respect for big reputations—and will bend over way, way backwards so as not to seem impressed when confronted with a celebrity.

I was really very glad to see him again although I did dread the effect his presence in our household would have on my work. As I came down the long hill to the railroad station I could see the train just pulling out.

Henry was waiting on the platform surrounded by a large pile of luggage. He had a small camera hanging from a strap around his shoulder.

He hurried over to the car. "What kind of shoes was he wearing?" he demanded without bothering to greet me. "Did he have boots on?"

"Did who have boots on?"

"Stanton, of course. Was he wearing hobnailed boots?"

"How the hell should I know? I didn't examine his feet."

"You found the body," he said accusingly. "You must have seen what he was wearing."

"I probably did, but I didn't notice whether he had on snowshoes or carpet slippers. Besides, what difference does it make?"

Henry sighed. "And I had always nourished the delusion that a scientific training taught people to observe. Didn't it occur to you that he might have left footprints?"

I shrugged my shoulders. "That's something for the police to worry about," I said. "Come on, let's get your bags in the car. I'm hungry and I want my breakfast. How did you get away?"

"Oh, I couldn't miss anything like this," he said cheerfully. "I sent a telegram to the office telling them that my four small nephews in the country were seriously ill. I'd have come out last night when I got your letter but I couldn't get a train at that hour."

"So you took the first one this morning?"

He nodded and hoisted a large wooden cabinet into the back of the car. "My photographic stuff," he explained. "Enlarger and everything."

"You have a new camera too, I see,"

"New model Leica with an f.2 lens. Wonderful little machine."

Henry spends enough money on cameras to support a colony of Chinese families in luxury. As soon as something new appears on the market he swaps in his old camera at a tremendous loss and acquires the most recent model. He possesses a vast knowledge of lenses, shutters, cameras, and equipment but he has absolutely no eye for taking a good picture. His photographs are masterpieces of technical virtuosity but they are somewhat less interesting than the snapshots you see in a drugstore window.

He climbed into the car and handed me a clipping from the morning paper. The story of the murder had been compressed into a few inches of space, and I was relieved to find that my name was not mentioned in connection with it. The killing of an obscure person in the country was of little interest to a metropolitan newspaper to which murders are a daily occurrence.

Henry started to shoot questions at me as we drove up the long rolling hills toward Brookdale. He jotted things down in an indecipherable script in a little notebook.

"How about the people in the tenant house—didn't they hear anything?" he asked.

The tenant house had been empty for almost two years, I explained. Stanton had put its last occupants out in the rain following a fearful quarrel over ground rights. He had rented them the house and then refused to allow his tenants to have an inch of soil in which to plant a garden.

"That tenant should be looked up," Henry said scrawling in his notebook. "Although, if he was going to kill Stanton he would probably have done it when he was turned out of his house. I suppose the police will follow up an obvious clue like that, though."

The police did investigate the tenant, I found out later. They discovered that he had moved to another part of the state and had the best of all possible alibis. He had been dead for more than a year, and his wife (who swore that her husband had met his death as the result of a cold caught when Stanton put them out in the rain) expressed unregenerate joy in hearing of Stanton's violent end. She, too, had an excellent alibi. She had been in a hospital at the time, suffering from malnutrition.

Henry kept questioning me as we drove along. Most of the things he asked seemed to me to be irrelevant and trivial, but I answered him with forbearing patience. He kept harping on motives. I tried to explain to him that almost everyone in Brookdale had at least one good reason to dislike Howard Stanton.

"That's not enough," he said. "People don't go around murdering someone just because they dislike him. There has to be something to crystallize their dislike into action strong enough to make them want to kill."

We stopped in Brookdale to pick up Emma. Henry was one of her favorite guests. She greeted him with excessive cordiality and got into the car with unusual spryness.

"I suppose you've told Mr. Hale all about our terrible tragedy?"

I nodded.

"Well," she said importantly, "another state trooper was here this morning to ask my opinion of the matter!"

Henry clucked appreciatively. "And what was your opinion?"

"I told him that it was murder right enough."

"You know you have no legal right to say that it was murder until the inquest has decided the matter," I told her. "You might get into trouble saying things like that."

She looked at me apprehensively for a moment, then she glanced at Henry and caught him winking. She simpered, turned to Henry, and went on:

"He asked me all about Howard—whether he had any enemies and such. I told him there were lots of people who didn't like Howard but they weren't the kind that would kill him. And I said that I was sure no one in Brookdale did it. It must have been strangers. They might have come in an automobile. Those city gangsters who take people for a ride might have come up here. They do terrible things."

Henry laughed. "You don't think they took Howard for a ride on his own tenant farm—or do you?"

"Not for a ride. But they might have killed him."

"Isn't it strange they didn't rob him?"

"Oh, those gangsters have lots of money."

"Well," said Henry, "it doesn't look like a gangsters' job to me. They don't go in for hand-to-hand fighting. It's too dangerous."

"I'm sure no one around here did it, though," she said firmly.

"What did you find out from the trooper?" Henry asked.

"He didn't seem to want to talk much," she admitted reluctantly. "He really didn't tell me anything new at all."

Joan had breakfast ready when we arrived. Henry greeted her in his best "I-kiss-the-hand-Madame" manner. I could see that he was trying to make up for his unduly hasty arrival. He presented her very ceremoniously with a package which, when unwrapped, proved to contain a bottle of Château Margaux 1920 and a large flask of crème de cacao.

Joan dismissed the wine casually. To her it was just another "sour" French wine. But she was glad to get crème
de cacao. She immediately forgave Henry, although I knew
that she was always put out when people dropped in on us
unexpectedly.

We were seated around a table on the back porch eating
breakfast when we heard a motorcycle come up the road.
Emma thrust her head through the kitchen window to tell
us that it was the same trooper who had questioned her
earlier in the morning.

"Here's our chance to get some information," Henry
whispered excitedly.

The trooper stomped heavily around the porch to where
we were sitting. I recognized him as the gum-chewing person who had stood guard over Hathaway and me on the
night of the murder. He greeted us with a gruff "Good
morning" and began abruptly: "I don't want to bother you
folks any more than I have to, but I'm supposed to ask you
some questions."

"A terrible thing, this murder," Henry said sententiously.

The trooper grunted. "I've seen worse."

"Has anybody been suspected?"

"Sure. The whole town." The trooper grinned. "This
Stanton guy didn't seem to have anything but enemies. It's
a wonder to me he lived as long as he did."

"But there must be some people who are more likely to
have done it than others," Henry insisted.

"That's just what we want to find out. But suppose I do
a little questioning now. That's what I'm here for."

He turned to me. "Your name's Whitby, isn't it? I saw
you when we found Stanton's body."

"That's right," I said eagerly, hoping that the police
were going to take over the responsibility for discovering
Stanton's corpse.

"Mm. And this is Mrs. Whitby, I suppose?"

Joan smiled sweetly.

"And you," he said turning to Henry, "do you live here too?"

"No," replied Henry promptly, "I'm just a visitor from New York. Got here this morning. My name is Henry Hale, and I live at 47 Mortimer Street, New York City."

The trooper grunted and addressed us: "Well, can any of you tell me anything at all about this business?"

Joan shook her head.

"I'm only a visitor," said Henry.

"I've already told you all I know about it," I hesitated and then said: "But how about having some breakfast with us?"

He accepted willingly. Over the coffee he became almost cordial.

"You know," he said, waving one of Emma's buns in the air, "there's a lot of people who think this business of running down a murderer is fun. Mostly, though, it's just asking a lot of questions and when you get your hands on somebody likely—you make him talk! There's been a lot more murders solved by a hunk of rubber hose than by all the microscopes and slick detectives you've read about."

"Do you ever read detective stories?" Henry inquired blandly.

"Sure," he said, "I read one once. About a guy who looked out of the window and spotted someone as a retired sergeant of marines just by looking at him."

"Ah, yes," breathed Henry, "Sherlock Holmes: *A Study in Scarlet.*"

"Yeah. That was it. Well, as I remember, he spotted him because the guy had an anchor tattooed on his hand, stood up straight like a soldier, and acted as if he was boss. Baloney! He might have been a doorman or a movie usher. My old woman's bossier than six generals. As to the tattoo, anybody might have that. I've got one myself." He pulled up his sleeve and showed us a full-rigged ship surrounded by a circle of stars.

"The only sailing I ever did was for flounders on Sunday. I had the tattoo put on when I was a kid in school."

"There weren't any movie ushers when Conan Doyle wrote that story," Henry objected mildly.

The trooper grunted through a mouthful of bun. When he had swallowed it he went on:

"A really smart guy who is out to kill somebody doesn't go through a lot of hocus-pocus. He kills his man quick when nobody is looking and beats it. If he doesn't plaster up everything with his fingerprints and has sense enough not to leave a lot of nice footprints around, the chances are a hundred to one he'll get away with it. He doesn't need an airtight alibi. How many people can prove just what they were doing at any special time? Murder's not so hard if you don't ball it up with a lot of movie stuff."

"What's your theory about this one?" asked Henry.

"I don't have theories. I just ask questions."

"They say that Stanton was strangled to death. It would take a pretty husky sort of murderer to do that, wouldn't it?"

"Might and might not. You'd be surprised how strong a little guy can be. Shorty—he's the smallest one in our outfit—can tear a phone book in half. I'd hate to have him get his paws on my throat."

He stood up and lit a cigarette.

"Well, I've got to run along. I've got a lot to do around this town yet. Thanks for the eats."

He sauntered off the porch, kicked his motorcycle engine into action, and was off in a burst of fire that sounded like a machine gun as it echoed back and forth between the hills.

"You certainly got a lot of information out of him," I told Henry.

Emma, standing behind the screen door, tittered softly.

CHAPTER V
THE CAT IN THE CHINA CLOSET

It was late when we finally got up from breakfast. Henry asked me to draw a map of the village for him which I did with great care and reasonable exactness. Brookdale derives its name from the fact that it is located where three brooks join together to make up one larger stream that flows south. Each of the contributing branches is named from the other three cardinal points of the compass. To the southeast of the village is a large, densely wooded hill known locally as the Mountain. It rises a thousand feet above sea level—not a very remarkable altitude as real mountains go, but it is the highest spot for many miles around.

The village is on fairly level ground but around it the neighboring hills rise like the walls of a natural amphitheater. The country is heavily covered with rather large second-growth timber. Although the section is only a few hours' journey from New York its isolation from railroads and main-traveled thoroughfares has tended to preserve its traditional rural atmosphere.

Brookdale was settled partly in the eighteenth century by a small group of people whose descendants still hold most of the land. And there is, of course, a small but constantly increasing number of city folk like ourselves who have bought property. Cordial enough relations exist between the natives and the invaders from the city, but actually the two groups mix very little—a fact which is probably due more to the standoffishness of city people than to any unfriendliness on the part of the natives.

The locality was an ideal one for my work. The rotting wood and piles of fallen leaves in the forest had yielded many specimens of the slime molds I was studying, and the long quiet hours of undisturbed peace that I enjoyed— before the Stanton murder—had enabled me to accomplish a great deal of work on my book. I had converted the little barn on our property into a laboratory, with a rather extensive herbarium file. When the murder broke I had been working on a fine specimen of *Enerthenema melanosperum* and I was eager to get back to it. The species is known but it had never before been observed in our part of the country.

Henry watched eagerly over my shoulder as I worked on the map. He was reasonably familiar with the neighborhood but I knew every foot of it, since my search for specimens had taken me over it many times. In fact, I must often have trespassed unknowingly on Stanton's precious acres but fortunately I had never been caught in the act.

Henry studied the map for a few minutes, then put it carefully away in his little notebook and suggested that we visit the scene of the murder. I should have preferred to work for a few hours before going to the inquest but I hadn't the heart to refuse Henry. Besides I wanted to get a good look at the place in the daytime.

We walked, down the road toward the village. The sun was shining brightly through the trees that overhung the road. I saw the brilliant flash of an oriole overhead and I could hear a catbird calling from some bushes nearby.

"Right now I'm missing a conference with a New England Yankee," Henry announced gleefully. "He's sure to be arguing about tenths of a cent. It's hard to understand how anyone as rich as that guy is can always be worrying about a tenth of a cent, but he does. Maybe that's why he's rich." Then he said: "I wonder if it would be possible for me to talk to everybody in Brookdale? There can't be so many people in a little town like this. How about taking me around and introducing me? I could lead up to the murder without being too obvious."

"Nothing doing," I said shortly. "I certainly am not going to help you annoy our neighbors."

"You don't want to have a murderer running at large around here, do you?"

"Not exactly. But I'm not going to drag you around to meet a lot of innocent people so you can plague them with your fool questions. The police seem to be doing quite well at it."

"All right," he said, still cheerful, "but when we do run into someone you can, as a matter of common courtesy, introduce me to him. Then it's just possible that he might want to talk about the murder of his own accord."

We came around a turn in the road and the first house of the village lay before us. It was a little square stone structure surrounded by a magnificent flower garden. Its owner was spraying some white roses.

"This gentleman, for instance, who is so sensibly cultivating his own garden. Who is he?"

"His name is Marigold," I said reluctantly. "I don't know much about him. He's a newcomer. He's had that place only a year or so. I haven't exchanged a dozen words with him."

"Well, why not get better acquainted? You might have a lot in common. He certainly a very capable gardener

"I don't want to know him. I've got—" I began desperately when Marigold saw us and stepped over to the fence waving his spray gun.

"Good morning, Professor," he said gaily. "It seems as though we are in for a little excitement. I hear you are going to be the star witness at the inquest."

I mumbled something and introduced Henry. Marigold shook hands with great enthusiasm.

"Nice roses you have," I said trying to change the subject. "Having trouble with them?"

"Just Japanese beetles. Why doesn't your precious agri-
cultural department do something about them?"

"It's not my department," I explained. "The State has
tried, but the natural philoprogenitiveness of Japanese
beetles seems to be a more effective force than any we can
find to get rid of them. Anyway, they're not as bad as they
used to be."

Marigold chuckled. He had a stout face that was burned
a deep tan. His gray hair contrasted curiously with the
dark color of his skin. He was wearing short white pants
that made him look somewhat absurd. His voice was high-
pitched and there was a distinctly feminine quality to his
gestures.

"Come in, gentlemen," he said, holding open the gate
to his garden, "come in and rest yourselves from the heat
of the sun and the dust of the road. Perhaps you would
like to have some iced tea? Ice spoils the true quality of
good tea and lemon ruins it altogether, but even so it
makes a refreshing drink on a hot day. I have a pitcher of
it in the icebox."

We sat down on some white garden chairs on a stone
terrace at the side of the house while Marigold went in to
get the tea. Henry stared around with great interest.

"I'm going to try and make this bird talk," he said in a
low voice. "Now, for the love of Mike, don't spoil my stuff."

Our host brought out a large crystal pitcher, some tall
glasses, and dainty colored squares of cloth for napkins.

"You'll like this tea," he told us. "I have it sent to
me from Darjeeling. There's nothing like Darjeeling tea.
The fresh air and oxygen of the Himalayas give it a fla-
vor which, gentlemen, is nothing less than magnificent. It
contains an extraordinary amount of vitamin B, I understand."

I grunted and tasted the tea. It seemed just like any
other tea. Henry became enthusiastic about it though, and
he and Marigold went into great detail about the relative

merits of Imperial Hyson, Soochong, and other varieties.
I shifted impatiently in my chair.

Suddenly I heard a faint scratching sound come from
somewhere inside the house. Henry and Marigold went on
talking. I heard the sound again. Then there was a crash
that sounded as though someone had upset a tray full of
glassware or crockery.

Marigold sprang out of his chair and rushed into the
house. A moment later he came out with a rueful expression on his face.

"The cat got into the china closet," he explained. "He
loves it in there for some reason I never can understand.
He knocked over half a dozen glasses. It doesn't matter
though. They aren't good glasses. You see, I have some
real Jacobean glassware and every time I hear the sound of
glass being broken I simply have heart failure."

"Where is the cat now?" Henry asked.

"He knows he's in disgrace and he's hiding from me. I
couldn't find him anywhere,"

"Why don't you call him?"

"It wouldn't be any use," Marigold said gravely. "He's
stone-deaf. Can't hear a thing. I think that's why he smash-
es so much glassware. He can't hear it crash, so it never
bothers him."

Henry looked at me and then changed the subject
abruptly.

"A terrible thing, this murder," he said. I wondered if
he was always going to begin in the same way.

"Murders are usually pretty terrible," said Marigold,
"but this one seems to have been particularly bad. It was
a crude, bungled job showing no sense or plan behind it.
I can understand a man committing a coldly premeditated
murder—in which case he usually does a neat, clean job of
the killing. This murder, however, was an absurdly slop-
py affair. The murderer killed his victim three times. He
choked him, he smashed his head, and then he hanged the

corpse. A great deal of lost motion, I should say, all for no ascertainable reason."

"He evidently had it in for Stanton and was just trying to express his hatred by inflicting such outrages on his dead body," I suggested.

"But there's no point to it, man," protested Marigold vigorously. "If he had hated Stanton so much he would want to make him suffer—while he was still alive. That I can understand. I can see the advantage of inflicting punishment on a living body by means which are novel and ingenious. But once Stanton was dead there was no use assaulting his unfeeling corpse. It was stupid. I have no use for such a murder. It lacks the finer technical points that distinguish a really first-rate performance."

"You seem to be something of a connoisseur," said Henry.

"In a way I am," Marigold said modestly. "Naturally I am interested only in the more unusual cases—cases that show some inventive genius, some brilliant imagination at work. Most of our modern murders seem to be rather prosaic affairs. The murderer nowadays is usually interested only in dispatching his victim as quickly as possible without exposing himself to detection. I admit to possessing an old-fashioned attachment to the more artistic performances of the past."

"Such as—" said Henry.

"Well, such as those the Orient was once noted for. Our Occidental murders like the poisonings of the Borgias, for instance, were rather dull. Any fool can give his guest poison and watch him die as a result of it. That requires no skill or exercise of the imaginative faculties. It takes the finer subtleties of the Oriental mind to devise really worthwhile means of making the human flesh suffer and the human mind quail. Even the best efforts of our medieval European torturers were, on careful analysis, somewhat repetitious and lacking in true inventiveness. The thumbscrew, the water torture, the rack, burning, breaking on the wheel, and so forth occur again and again with painful regularity. No, you must look to the East for anything really good. Take, for instance, the torture of the hungry rat that the Chinese were so fond of—that, gentlemen, was really ingenious!"

"What was it?" I inquired innocently.

"It was very simple," explained Marigold. "The victim was seated upon an iron pot containing a rat. He was strapped to the pot and could not move. Eventually—after a day or two of horrible suspense for the victim—the rat got hungry. There was only one way for him to satisfy both his hunger and his desire to escape. Rather clever, isn't it?" he asked with a genial smile.

"You are familiar with the torture of the wet hides, I suppose?" Henry asked casually.

"Oh, quite, but it was so crude," said Marigold, dismissing the subject contemptuously. "Now take the Persian method—the one that Artaxerxes II used upon Mithridates. That was really good."

"The torture of the boats, you mean?" Henry said promptly.

Marigold seemed disappointed that Henry had heard of it. He renounced his nostalgic admiration for tortures of the past and launched into a speculative monologue on the possibilities that modern science could bring to the technique of inflicting pain.

"Electricity has been used for capital punishment," he said enthusiastically, "but think what could be done with it if instead of using this terrific force simply to cause a relatively quick and easy death, our research men really applied themselves to discover new ways to blast the nerves, disrupt the normal function of the brain, flay the delicate membranes of—"

I had had enough. I practically forced Henry out of the garden. Our host followed us disconsolately to the gate.

"Must you really go?" he said regretfully. "I did want to show you what I have been doing to some mountain laurel that I transplanted."

"Do you use fire or boiling oil?" Henry asked solemnly.

I urged Henry along before our host could have a chance to reply.

"By the way," I called back from the road, "do you know they're poisonous?—the laurel leaves, I mean."

"Oh yes, yes indeed," he said beaming. "I know all about that."

"There are damned few people who do," I muttered to Henry as soon as we were far enough away. "Your Mr. Marigold seems to know all about lots of things."

"Doesn't he?" Henry said thoughtfully.

"It certainly will be delightful to have such an erudite and cultured gentleman for a neighbor. I wonder if he raises aconite and *Cicuta maculata,* too?"

"What is *Cicuta maculata?*"

"Water hemlock—the most violently poisonous plant found on this continent."

"That's nice to know," Henry said. "You learn a lot playing around with murder. For years I thought aconite was some kind of explosive, but reading mystery stories cleared that up. Mountain laurel is common enough, though. There's plenty of it in the woods around here."

"It's common enough all right," I agreed. "But fortunately very few people are as well informed about its toxic qualities as our gentle friend seems to be."

"Mr. Marigold is evidently an exceptional person. Even his cat, with its penchant for smashing china, is out of the run of ordinary felines. I'd like to see that cat. I'd like very much to see it. I just want to find out whether it has four legs or. . . ."

"Or what?"

"Or two."

CHAPTER VI
"BY PERSON OR PERSONS UNKNOWN"

I was surprised to find that there were not more than a dozen people gathered around the entrance to the Stanton tenant farm. The condition of the place, however, made it plain that it had already been overrun by a mob of curiosity seekers. I noticed that someone had hacked off and taken away the branch of the sycamore from which Stanton's body had been hanged.

Henry looked around in disgust. He suggested that we examine the hay field where Stanton had been working. Even the short stumble there had been trampled down in the area near the brook. Nevertheless Henry was determined to go over it carefully and he kept snapping pictures of everything in the vicinity. I wandered over to a group of sightseers and started a conversation with Henry Morton, the meek and subjugated husband of our W.C.T.U. leader. He is a gray little man with a mustache that is much too big for him. He has a curious habit of looking around before he speaks. I suppose he wants to make sure that his wife is not within hearing distance.

"You knew Howard Stanton pretty well, didn't you?" I asked casually.

"Guess so," he said, spitting into the brook. "I was in the army with him. I picked him up when he fell down on San Juan Hill."

"I didn't know he had been wounded in the war."

"Wounded? Who said anything about his being wounded? His horse got scared when it heard firing and threw Howard off on his behind. Knocked him right out, it did. I picked him up, put him on my horse, and carried him back of the lines. The real fighting didn't begin till a couple of hours later. Howard missed it all. He never was much of a hand with horses. They didn't seem to take to him."

"You must have been friendly with him then. You practically saved his life."

"Friendly hell," said Morton in his mild low voice. "He lent me fifty dollars once on a sixteen-acre woodlot. And then he cut every stick of wood off it. Said the wood just paid the interest. Howard was a friendly sort, all right." He spit disgustedly in the brook again.

"What was he like when he was in the army?"

"He was the fightingest soldier I ever did see except when there was any real fighting to do. He'd roar into a saloon, pound his fist on the bar, and yell for drinks. But when it came time to pay the bill he was so quiet you could hear a feather drop on a sofa cushion. He was made a corporal once and he started to act tough but the men in his squad caught him one night and the next morning he sort of resigned the job. At least he tried to."

"Doesn't anyone ever have a good word to say for him?"

"What is there to say?" Morton asked very practically.

I saw Henry approaching, so I excused myself hastily and went to meet him.

"Did you find anything?" I asked.

He held out for my inspection a twisted horseshoe nail and an ancient metal button from somebody's overalls.

"No arrowheads?" I asked. "There ought to be some arrowheads around here. There used to be Indians in this part of the country."

"Go to hell," he said abstractedly. "These things probably don't mean anything but then again they might. You can't expect to find your clues all neatly labeled."

He put his finds away in his pocket.

"Let's walk up toward the Stanton farmhouse. I'd like to see just exactly how far it is from here," he suggested.

We walked slowly toward the road. Henry was obviously concentrating on something.

"Well, Maestro, what now?"

He stopped and said out loud: "Forty-seven. Don't bother me. I'm trying to pace the exact distance."

Henry walked on with measured steps. I followed leisurely.

"One hundred and twenty-two paces," he announced as we came opposite the driveway leading into the Stanton farm. "That makes a little over three hundred feet."

"Amazing!"

He ignored me and looked carefully at the large white house with its wreath of funeral flowers on the door.

"When is he going to be buried?"

"Tomorrow afternoon, I believe."

"Do you suppose we could attend the funeral?"

"I daresay it could be managed. Why do you want to go?"

"I'd like to get a look at the deceased. I never saw the gentleman and I want to know what he looked like. Besides, I'd be interested in seeing how everyone acts. You never can tell what might happen."

We started back toward the village. The inquest was due to start in a short time. It was to be held in the meeting room of the local hotel. Years ago, before the automobile had made the town so easily accessible to New York, this building had really been a hotel; it holds the title only by courtesy now. The owner uses the place as his home and rents out the former dining room for township committee meetings and other matters of public business.

It was evident that all the people assembled in front of the place could never get inside. A trooper stood at the door. As a witness I was naturally permitted to enter, and I persuaded the trooper to let me take Henry in, too.

Joan was already inside, waiting for us in one of the front-row seats. Mr. Marigold was sitting next to her, and I noticed that Joan was carrying a large bunch of white roses from his garden.

"I started to walk here," she said. "Mr. Marigold gave me a lift—and some iced tea. Wasn't that nice of him?"

"How did you get in?" I asked.

"It's a public affair, isn't it? I'd like to see anyone keep me out!"

I sat down and glanced around the low-ceilinged room. There was a constant murmur of voices. It seemed to me that everyone in Brookdale was there. I saw Mrs. Denner and Stanton's brother, the doctor. Joe Fammel waved to me cordially. George Hathaway succeeded in catching my eye and he grinned at me with a silly and frightened smile.

Hathaway was the first witness called. He was evidently determined to tell as little as possible, probably on the theory that the less he said, the less he was likely to incriminate himself. The coroner once or twice almost lost his temper when Hathaway became confused about a matter of time. Time, the coroner said, with some mistaken notion of legal terminology, was of the essence in this case. Would the witness please make up his mind whether it was half an hour, or an hour after his return from the hayfield that he had started out to search for Stanton? Hathaway finally admitted that it was probably an hour, and the coroner, with as much satisfaction as if he had wrung a confession of guilt from the witness, finally permitted him to step down.

I was called next. The coroner was much gentler with me. I told without any prompting the all-too-familiar story of my encounter with Hathaway on the night of the murder and of our subsequent discovery of the body.

Then the coroner began to question me.

"Did you observe the condition of the blood on the body of the deceased? Was it still fresh—or had it coagulated?"

"The blood was still dripping from the body, so it was evidently still fresh."

"Was the body still warm?"

"I didn't touch it."

"You have just told us that you ran into it in the darkness as you were crossing the bridge."

"The corpse was clothed. I didn't notice its temperature."

"Had *rigor mortis* set in?"

"No. But I have already said that blood was dripping from the corpse. It's hardly likely that blood would flow freely if—"

"That will be all, Mr. Whitby. Thank you."

I returned to my seat convinced that rural coroners just ask questions at random because they have no idea of what they should try to find out. Stanton had admittedly been seen alive by George Hathaway only an hour before we found his body, and the medical testimony of the coroner's physician would bring out all there was to be said about the physical condition of the corpse, so the questions asked me were obviously unnecessary.

Captain Macready was delivering a speech to the jury. He had done this and he had done that. He had left no stone unturned. He had done everything but actually find the murderer, and that, he implied, was something that he would do very shortly. But he contributed nothing that I did not already know.

At last Dr. Sampson, the coroner's physician, was put on the stand—actually brought forward to the coroner's table, that is. In a clear, dry voice he outlined the only new evidence that had been revealed at the inquest.

He told how he had examined the body of Howard Stanton *in situ,* and how he had later performed an autopsy on it.

"The body was still warm when I arrived," he said. "The time of the murder as established by previous witnesses is entirely reasonable. Death was clearly caused by strangulation. The throat of the victim was seized from behind by someone with a powerful grip. From the general condition of the body and the appearance of the throat itself, a struggle evidently had taken place between the victim and his murderer. When the murderer finally removed his hands from his victim's throat, death had already occurred. The larynx had been fractured and respiration must have ceased. The smashing in of the victim's skull occurred immediately afterwards, I should think. And then, although it must have been evident even to a layman that life was extinct, the murderer hanged the dead body from a tree. I should like to point out that he made quite a professional hangman's job of it. The knot in the rope was correctly made and placed. Also—and this is indeed curious—the neck of the murdered man was broken. His assassin did not simply place a rope around his neck and haul him up in the tree. He must have staged a formal hanging of his victim, for the snapped cervical vertebrae indicate that the body must have been dropped from a fairly considerable height!"

There was quite a stir in the little meeting room. The coroner rapped on the table for attention.

"Do you have any idea how the body could have been dropped?"

"The rope used for hanging had its other end tied fast to the timbers of the bridge. It would have been a simple matter to pull the body up tight to the branch of the tree and then let it drop so the rope could run freely over the branch. The end of the rope made fast to the bridge would serve to bring the falling body to a sudden stop in midair. A drop of about ten feet could have been arranged in this way. Mr. Stanton was a very heavy man. He weighed two hundred and eight pounds. Such a drop might very well have broken the neck of his inanimate body."

There was very little left to be said after that. One of the troopers testified that the stone used in the murder

had been found on the edge of the brook. There was still
some hair and slight traces of blood on it but the water
had prevented any clear fingerprints from remaining as
evidence. He also brought out that no footprints had been
found.

The murderer had evidently waded along the shallow
brook and emerged at the log bridge. The troopers had
made a careful search of the banks of the little stream but
its rocky borders had yielded nothing. Mrs. Denner was
then called upon to testify but her tight-lipped monosyl-
lables revealed little if anything of interest.

The jury quickly came to a verdict of "willful murder by person or persons unknown." The inquest was adjourned and I, for one, was glad to be out in the open
air again. People collected in little groups in front of the
hotel, talking eagerly about the thrice-murdered corpse.

"It wasn't very exciting," said Joan disappointedly.

"Oh, I wouldn't say that," Marigold protested, "That
part about the actual hanging of the corpse was rather
good, I thought. I was afraid that the murderer had just
tied a rope around Stanton's neck and slung him up in the
tree. There seems to be some slight trace of imagination
about this murder, after all."

"It doesn't bring them any nearer to finding who the
murderer is, though," Joan said. "There was no really new
evidence brought out."

"Oh, well, an inquest in a case like this doesn't mean
much; it just starts the legal ball rolling. The whole thing
is only a formal way of assuring the public that the deceased is really dead and met his death by foul means,"
Henry explained. "And Mr. Marigold is certainly right
about the business of hanging the corpse. It tells us something about the psychological make-up of the murderer."

I was eager to get away from the village and its gossip
as quickly as possible. Marigold volunteered to drive us
back to the house and I promptly accepted his invitation.
Henry suddenly slipped away from us. I saw him talking

with the trooper who had breakfasted with us. He beckoned to us to go on, so Joan and I got into the back seat of Marigold's big sedan.

When we arrived at our house Tinkel greeted us with wild enthusiasm and tried to lick Marigold's face when he was presented to her. He took her into his arms and examined her carefully.

"She's going to be in heat soon," he said, poking her belly.

Joan took the dog from him.

"Mm. That'll be nice. We'll have every dog in the neighborhood coming around to call."

"You'd better be careful," he said solemnly. "Dachshunds must never be mixed. They make perfectly outrageous combinations with other breeds."

"Yes, I saw one once," Joan said. "All mixed up with an Airedale. He seemed to be awfully unhappy. But won't you come in and see our house?"

We went into the house. Marigold and Joan began to discuss curtain material. It seemed that he was having a problem choosing color combinations or cloth or some such thing. This went on for some time.

"Shall I make something to drink?" I suggested at last.

"Oh, yes, do," Joan urged. "We have some wonderful crème de cacao, Mr. Marigold. Will you have an angel's tip?"

"A what? Oh, yes—by all means. I should love to have one."

I went to the kitchen to prepare the drinks and mixed myself some Scotch and soda. Joan and Marigold were seated on steamer chairs on the porch by the time I had the drinks ready. They were talking about patchwork quilts. I downed my Scotch hurriedly, excused myself, and went to the laboratory. I worked until late in the afternoon.

CHAPTER VII
THE THING IN THE BROOK

About five o'clock my eyes began to get tired. I stowed the microscope away under a bell jar and stuck my manuscript in the desk.

I went back to the house. Marigold, much to my relief, had already gone and Henry was sitting on the porch talking to Joan. I asked him for a cigarette and found there wasn't one anywhere in the house.

Dinner wasn't due for nearly two hours, so I suggested to Henry that we go to the village to get some cigarettes. He wanted to walk but I thought it might be easier to avoid another meeting with Marigold if we took the car. I turned Bertha around and we headed for the village.

We stopped at Joe Fammel's store. Several men were sitting on the high old-fashioned porch. I nodded to them and asked Joe to get the cigarettes. We stayed in the car while he went in for them. Ramsey Morgan, who was among the men on the porch, leaned down toward us and said in what was intended to be a confidential whisper:

"Whiskey Joe was here a little while ago talking sort of wild about Howard Stanton's murder."

Henry brightened.

"What did he say?"

"It didn't make, much sense. Joe was even drunker than usual. He just kept saying something about Howard's being killed by a beast instead of a man. A big animal that he'd heard splashing in the brook."

"Did he see it?"

"He didn't say. But then I guess Joe sees a lot of queer animals sometimes."

The men on the porch laughed appreciatively.

"I never heard tell of any animal around here that could strangle a man," one of them said skeptically.

"And then smash his head in with a rock and hang him!" Morgan added.

"Whiskey had ought to watch what he's saying, though."

"Yes, sir, he's likely to get the blame for that murder laid right down on his own doorstep."

"Has anyone told the state troopers what he said?" Henry asked.

"Guess not," Morgan said. "He hasn't been gone more than a few minutes and there haven't been any troopers around since he left."

"Which way did he go?"

"Back to his shack, I guess. But he was so drunk I ain't sure if he ever got there."

"Come on," urged Henry, grasping my arm. "Let's hear what he has to say."

I paid Joe for the cigarettes and hurriedly backed the car around.

The path to Whiskey Joe's shack leaves the main road a little beyond the farmhouse occupied by David Hamlin and his sister. It rises steadily as it almost parallels the shore of the North Brook for about a hundred feet.

"He might have seen or heard something," Henry pointed out. "This path is certainly very near the spot where Stanton was killed and you can see the brook clearly from here."

"It must have been almost dark when the murderer went past here though," I objected.

"I don't suppose he really saw him well enough to recognize him, but he might have some information for us that would be useful. What sort of person is Whiskey Joe, anyway?"

"The town drunkard—as you may have guessed. Indigent, lazy, and a fabulous liar—but a perfectly swell guy. One of those rare people who remain sweetly good-natured even when completely pie-eyed. You know the old saying—everybody's friend and his own worst enemy."

Henry nodded and walked on.

"There he is," he said suddenly. "Passed out, I guess."

Whiskey Joe lay on the path only a few feet ahead of us. He had rolled over so that he was lying face upward. A ray of late afternoon sunlight coming through a break in the trees was shining in his eyes, but he was unconscious of it. He was dead-drunk.

"We'd better carry him to his shack," I said.

We lifted him up and carried him across the fields. The door of his ramshackle dwelling was swaying gently in the wind. We put him down on the bed. His body sprawled across the dirty blankets. He muttered something indistinctly. No amount of shaking could get any further response from him. We decided to leave him there.

"I think we'd better phone the police," Henry said. "They ought to be here when he comes to."

Henry telephoned from Fammel's store to the local state police station. He told them what he had heard about Whiskey Joe's story. They were not certain how soon they could have a man available to come to Brookdale, so they asked us to wait in the town until he arrived.

I suggested to Henry that we drop in on Edgar Harmon, one of our neighbors who had been confined to bed for several years as the result of a stroke which had paralyzed his legs. Conversation was one of the few pleasures left to him and he was always pathetically glad to see visitors. I had known him for some time and Henry had often gone with me to visit him. His house was across the road from Fammel's store.

The place had been neglected of late, for Harmon, of course, could no longer take care of it. His wife had committed suicide after having given birth to a child who had proved to be mentally defective. This child, now a man past thirty, was a harmless and good-natured imbecile. His name was Emmett. He was, I admit, a repulsive-looking creature. He had been afflicted with paralysis which drew his face to one side in a perpetual grimace. His right arm was useless, with the fingers of the hand clenched stiffly, and he spoke a guttural language of his own which only his father could interpret easily. I had tried several times to help Harmon out by giving his son some manual work to do. He had whitewashed our cellar for us, cleaned up the grounds, and mowed the lawn in a haphazard fashion. He was thoroughly undependable, though. A butterfly or a soaring bird would distract him so that he would drop his work and wander off somewhere without bothering to return.

Obviously such a person was unable to take charge of his father and the house. Harmon was, I suppose, too poor to be able to afford a regular attendant. Miss Harvey, the elderly spinster whom I have already mentioned, looked after him to the extent of cooking his meals and doing a little desultory housekeeping.

For someone whose life had been touched with so much tragedy, Harmon was remarkably cheerful. He was, I am certain, the best-educated person in Brookdale. He read a great deal and manifested a lively interest in current affairs.

He was reading a newspaper when we came in and his immediate concern was more with the state of affairs in Germany than with the murder which had startled his native village. Henry, of course, wanted to discuss the Stanton case rather than Hitler, and he quickly steered the conversation back to Brookdale.

"You knew Howard Stanton, I suppose," Henry began.

"Of course," the invalid answered. "We were in the army together. I can't say that I've been very intimate with him since then. He wasn't exactly a sociable sort, you know."

Henry nodded. "I've gathered as much. Apparently everybody around here seems to have had some cause to want to do away with him. There's no lack of suspects. Too many of them, in fact. There's something in the wind now, though."

"We seem to be on the track of a clue," I explained, and told Harmon of Whiskey Joe's babbling.

"I wouldn't put too much hope in finding out anything from Joe," Harmon said. "He's all right when he's sober, but his alcoholic imagination has filled these quiet hills with more queer animals than you could find in a circus."

"So I've been told," Henry said. "But we can't afford to overlook any bets. Have you any theory of your own about the murder?"

"No, I can't say that I have," Harmon answered slowly. "All my contact with life is second-hand now, and I've found that the affairs of the world at large are more interesting than local gossip. The German situation, for instance, is something I follow from day to day. . . ."

Henry gave up the attempt to find out anything more about the murder and the conversation dwelt on European politics for some time. We stayed until Miss Harvey began to bustle about in the kitchen, making sounds that warned us that she had dinner ready. Harmon invited us to return to his house for a game of three-handed pinochle while we waited for the trooper. Pinochle was his one social diversion.

We went back to our own house to get a hurried dinner. Then we started out again for the village. Henry suggested that we stop at Whiskey Joe's shack to see if he had come to. I thought that one of us ought to be at Harmon's in case the trooper should arrive, so I dropped Henry off at the crossroads and arranged for him to meet me at the Harmon house. It was rather surprising to me that the police were taking their own time about sending anyone, but they evidently did not attach much importance to what we had told them.

Harmon was instructing his son to arrange a card table so we could play. The rapport between the two was marvelous. The gangling idiot, under the guidance of the father, was able to carry out instructions almost as well as a normal person could.

Harmon had been reading something in the paper about Concord and Walden Pond. He began to talk about Thoreau, who was a great favorite of his. His son sat quietly in a far corner of the room, watching us with eyes that stared blankly through the deepening twilight.

"When Thoreau died—in fact I might say by the end of the Civil War—the best of America had ceased to exist," Harmon said earnestly. "Lincoln was dead and John Brown had been hanged. The age of heroes had passed and the age of the money-grubbers began. America no longer stood for democracy and freedom—it was only a place to be despoiled and exploited. Thoreau lived and died at the right time. I often wish I had been born in that era instead of in these fearful times." He smiled grimly. "Although, I don't suppose it matters much when one lives—in this condition."

I was always embarrassed when Harmon referred to his affliction. I tried to steer the conversation back to safer channels.

"The first half of the nineteenth century was an exciting time from my point of view," I said, feeling as though I were delivering a classroom lecture. "Darwin was working on his *Origin of Species;* botanical classification was seriously being undertaken—"

"Yes, Professor," Harmon said pleasantly, playing up to my leading remark, "and the whole fascinating field of fungi was practically unexplored."

"Well, not exactly. Linnaeus, of course, had almost ignored it, but Schaeffer, Batsch, Leers, Bulliard, and others had laid the ground work even in the eighteenth century."

I heard Henry's footsteps on the porch with some relief. He knocked at the screen door and came in.

"How is he?" I asked eagerly.

"The same. I don't think he's moved a muscle since we left him. He's breathing more naturally, though."

The idiot boy stirred restlessly in his chair.

"You don't have to wait up, Emmett," Harmon said in a gentle voice. "Lie down on the couch if you're tired."

Without a word the boy got up and stretched himself out heavily on the couch that stood in the far end of the big room.

"Would you mind lighting the lamp?" Harmon said. "We may as well begin our game."

CHAPTER VIII
THE PATTERN REPEATS

It was just after dark when we finally heard the noisy sputter of a motorcycle. Henry had been winning with a series of astounding hands. He got up almost reluctantly and opened the door to let in our tattooed trooper.

"Sorry to be so late, folks," he said grinning at us. "I was supposed to have this night off. I was all ready to take the old lady to the movies when the chief phoned me."

Henry and I got into our car and led the police motorcycle through the darkness. In a few minutes we arrived at the place where the path to Whiskey Joe's shack left the road. The trooper stopped and stood up his motorcycle. I took my own small flashlight. The trooper had a very powerful one. We walked quickly up the path.

Suddenly our escort stopped, switched off his light, and signaled to me to do the same. We stood there under the trees, in almost total darkness.

"Did you hear anything?" he whispered tensely.

I stood still and listened. I could hear nothing but the incessant chorus of millions of insects that were serenading the summer night.

"Let's go slow," the trooper advised in a low tone, "and without lights. I think I heard someone."

We proceeded cautiously through the darkness for the few hundred feet that separated us from the shack. It stood on a level plateau in a clear field beyond the woods. As we came out from under the trees I could see the dim outlines of the building. The door was open and it creaked slightly in the wind as it swung to and fro.

Henry stopped us and whispered: "I closed the door when I left. Latched it, too. Funny it's open now."

The trooper went ahead hurriedly. As we arrived in front of the shack he snapped on his light and turned its bright rays into the dark interior. I could make out the form of Whiskey Joe still lying on the bed. The trooper plunged into the shack ahead of us. We followed.

I heard him curse. At first I couldn't make out what he saw, and then I noticed that although Whiskey Joe was still lying as we had left him, there was a heavy stone where his head rested.

And around it was a darkening stain that was spreading even as we watched!

I shall never forget that close, dark room with its frightful occupant. The trooper had dashed abruptly out of the shack, leaving us there in the feeble gleam of my flashlight.

Henry took the light, bent over the bed, and drew a long breath. The body was a horrible sight. The head had been hideously smashed by the big stone and around the neck, tied in a hangman's noose, was a short length of rope!

Henry pointed significantly at the throat—there were bruises there—evidently made by human fingers. He ran the light quickly over the corpse. The blue shirt had been torn open, exposing Whiskey Joe's thin white chest. The skin was spattered with blood, and I noticed curiously that there was a faint reddish circle on the left side. The blood everywhere was very fresh. It gleamed darkly in the dull glow of the searchlight. It had even stained the rope that hung from the neck of the corpse.

I tugged at Henry's arm.

"We don't have to stay in here—with this, do we?" I asked anxiously.

"Go on. Wait outside if you want to," Henry said. "I'm going to try to make a photograph with the light of this searchlight."

"You can't possibly. It isn't strong enough."

"I can try," he said. "I have an f.2 lens on my camera, and I can take a time exposure."

I went out in the cool darkness outside. There was no moon but the stars twinkled brightly overhead. I stood there and wondered whether I had some natural affinity for murdered corpses. This was the second one in two days now.

I could hear the trooper trampling through the brush. In a few minutes Henry came out of the house.

"Do you think you got a picture?" I asked.

"I hope so," he said, putting his camera back in his pocket. "It will probably be rather faint, but with an intensifier I may be able to get a printable image. Have you got some potassium bichromate?"

"I guess so."

The bright gleam of the trooper's searchlight was rapidly approaching us.

"Missed him," he said. "I saw the lights of his car but he pulled out in a hurry. Is there a road back there?"

"There's a sort of road. It's pretty bad but a car could come through by way of Rocky Hill."

"Okay. I'm going to have a try for him." He started to run. "Phone headquarters for me. Tell 'em to send some men up," he called back over his shoulder as he moved toward his motorcycle.

"What name shall I give them?" Henry yelled after him. "What's your name?"

"Anderson. Nick Anderson," he said and disappeared in the darkness.

"Has Harmon got a phone?" Henry asked me.

"No. We'll have to bother Joe Fammel again. He's probably in bed by now. They go to bed early around here."

"No matter. We'll have to wake him up. Come on, let's go."

We ran back to the car and I drove so quickly over the bumpy road that I narrowly missed sending the car into a tree.

"Now don't act like Paul Revere," I warned Henry. "We don't have to wake up the whole town."

He knocked quietly on the door of the Fammel house. There was no answer.

I threw some pebbles against the window of the room where Joe and his wife slept. Someone moved about in there and then I heard Mrs. Fammel say in a low, tense voice: "Don't open the door, Joe. It might be that murderer."

"It's all right," I said. "It's me. Jim Whitby. We want to use your phone. Something's happened."

Joe's voice answered me. He mumbled that he'd be down. Presently he opened the door and stood there for a moment blinking at us. He was wearing an old-fashioned nightshirt.

"What's the matter?"

"There's been another murder," Henry told him hurriedly. "Whiskey Joe's been killed. I want to call the state police.

Joe stared his surprise. Several precious minutes passed before we could get him back into the house to draw on a pair of trousers. Then he led the way to the store which is alongside the house. He snapped on the lights and the homely old-fashioned interior with its rows of canned goods and bright fresh vegetables gave me a comforting sense of security again.

Henry turned the hand crank to ring the operator.

"I want state police headquarters at Fammelton," I heard him say. Then he turned to me. "Maybe you'd better talk to them," he suggested. "You're a resident."

I shook my head. "Go on, the pleasure's all yours."

"Hello. State police? This is Henry Hale speaking from Fammel's store in Brookdale. Trooper Anderson asked me to call you. There's been another murder. Yes, another murder. Just like Stanton's. Head bashed in with a stone and a rope around the neck."

There was a pause. Henry turned to Joe Fammel. "What was Whiskey Joe's real name?"

"Hartram," he said. "Joseph Hartram."

"Joseph Hartram," repeated Henry dutifully. "All right. We'll wait here for you."

He hung up the phone.

"They want us to wait here for them," he told Fammel. "Do you mind?"

"No, of course not. I'll get some more clothes on and keep you company."

"You'd better leave the light on in here so they can spot the store when they arrive."

"I'll do better than that," Fammel said. He switched on the big white lights in front of the store. "Make yourselves at home. I'll be back as soon as I can calm down the missus."

Henry and I sat down on the long bench on the porch.

"Well," observed Henry jauntily. "I guess I'm right in the middle of a murder case now all right."

I assured him, fervently, that he was.

CHAPTER IX
UNLEASH THE HOUNDS!

About half an hour after we had telephoned the police, I heard the faint sound of a siren coming through the hills. A few minutes later two motorcycles roared in, followed by a big touring car. Several men in uniform leaped out and came toward us.

Captain Macready greeted me with some surprise.

"You in on this again?"

"It looks that way," I said unhappily. "Let me introduce you to Mr. Hale, though. He found the body this time. I just happened to be along."

"That's what you said last time," he said and turned to Henry.

"What's the story?"

Henry explained.

"Get the coroner on the phone and tell him he's got another job," the captain told Fammel. "Come on, let's get going."

We led our police escort back to the path to Whiskey Joe's shack. As we climbed up the hill Henry continued his story to the captain. When we arrived at the shack the captain flashed his light on the bed, leaned over and gingerly felt the body.

"He certainly hasn't been dead long. He's still warm. Let's get a light in here."

One of the troopers lit the kerosene lamp that served as the only source of illumination. Its faint rays emphasized the darkness of the room. The body lay enshrouded in deep shadow.

"All right, Hamilton, you make the search. The rest of you can wait outside," the captain told us. "And don't trample all over the ground." Through the open door I could see Hamilton, the only man in the police party who was not in uniform, carefully going over the room with a searchlight. Some more troopers came up with two powerful electric lamps. The captain approached us. The scar on his forehead stood out lividly. He drew out a cigar, bit off the tip, and thrust it into his mouth without making any attempt to light it.

"You were the last one to see this man alive. Is that right?" he said, addressing Henry.

"Yes," said Henry evenly, "except for the murderer, I probably was."

"What time was it when you saw him?"

"About eight o'clock, I should say," Henry answered, turning to me for confirmation. I nodded silently.

"You're sure he was all right then?"

"I shook him to see if he could be waked up. I couldn't very well have missed that stone and the blood and the rope. It was still fairly light then."

The captain grunted. "Do you live around here?"

"No," Henry said. "I'm from New York. I'm visiting Mr. Whitby."

"I see. Well, Mr. Whitby, can you add anything to what your friend has told me?"

"Not very much, I'm afraid," I admitted. "Mr. Hale has explained that Trooper Anderson, who was with us when we discovered the body, heard a car start up on the Rocky Hill road a few hundred feet behind the house. It might be worthwhile to examine that road, although I suppose you can't expect to find much."

"There might be tire tracks," the captain said. "Suppose you take one of my men over there and show him the road."

He singled out a trooper to go with me.

"Take the main road around. I don't want any more tracks made through the brush."

We took one of the big searchlights with us but our search was fruitless. The Rocky Hill road was, logically enough, hard and stony, affording little chance for a car to leave any tire impressions.

"We might pick up something when its daylight," the trooper who accompanied me said. "We could close this road off so no one could come through to make any more tracks. The road isn't much used anyway, is it?"

"No, it isn't, and you can detour any cars that might want to come through by having them take another road that branches off at a concrete bridge about half a mile back."

We walked back to join the others. Anderson was there, talking to the captain.

"Did he get the car?" I asked Henry eagerly.

"No, no luck. It had too much of a start. It must have gone north though, or he'd have seen it coming down this way."

"There are a dozen roads up that way that it might have taken," I said. "I guess that's that."

"We should have stuck right here all evening with Whiskey Joe," Henry remarked regretfully. "If we'd stayed here Joe would be alive now and we would probably have the murderer. It's evident that he did know something about it—too much for his own good, I guess."

I nodded and wandered over to the captain. "I don't know how you feel about laymen butting into police business," I said, "but I'd like to suggest something that might help—"

"Let's hear about it," he said, almost genially. "We're always willing to hear suggestions even if we don't always take 'em."

"I suppose the trooper who went to search the Rocky Hill road with me has already informed you that we didn't find anything. He told me you could close the road off and make a careful inspection of it in the daytime."

The captain nodded. "Sure, we'll do that all right."

"What I want to suggest is this: There's a man here in the village who is quite a woodsman. I've often gone hunting with him. He has a well-trained dog—no blood-hound—just a mutt, but he can follow a trail. If you think it advisable I could get him up here and let him have a try at it."

"Not a bad idea," said the captain. "We might even pick up some footprints. The dog might help. Go ahead. Get him."

"Who's the mighty hunter?" Henry asked as we walked through the dark path leading to the road.

"Cal Smith. You know him."

"Sure," he said approvingly. "I remember him. He's a good guy."

"Yes, and he was a pal of Joe's. He'll probably be glad to get a chance to help run down Joe's murderer."

Caleb Smith was our nearest neighbor. He lived alone in a little house surrounded by a large and beautifully kept truck garden from which he made a precarious living by selling vegetables to summer residents. He was a great hunter—fishing was too tame for him, even though the streams around Brookdale were famous for their trout. He owned an old army Krag of which he was very proud, and an ancient double-barreled shotgun of the open-hammer type.

He was a really fine marksman. I have seen him take a twenty-two rifle and smash bottle after bottle thrown into the air. I can do this trick myself in an amateur sort of way, but I could never make twenty and thirty perfect shots in succession as he can.

He and his dog—which he said was mostly beagle, al-though it evidently had plenty of other strains as well—were inseparable. Horace was an unfriendly beast, the ter-ror of the other dogs in the neighborhood, and the nemesis of countless rabbits and pheasants.

Horace was supposed to know me, but he greeted me with a deep menacing growl as I stopped the car in front of Smith's house.

"You get out and knock on the door," said Henry. "That hound ought to know you well enough not to bite."

"He does—in the daytime," I retorted, and honked vigorously on the horn.

Smith stuck his head out of the window. "Will you come down," I said politely, "and take this damned dog away? Something's happened. We're going to need your assistance in a little midnight hunting."

Smith appeared in trousers hastily drawn over his nightshirt. He snapped a leash on Horace's collar. The dog quieted down immediately.

I explained the details of the murder. Smith listened in silence. Then he swore softly.

"I'll be ready soon as I get my clothes on," he said finally.

"I'll come back for you," I told him. "I'm going up to see how my wife is. She's all alone."

There was a light in our living room but the house was locked tightly. I hammered at the door. Joan appeared presently, peering apprehensively through a window.

"That's a hell of a way to treat me," she complained bitterly as she opened the door. "Leaving me here all alone with a murderer prowling around."

"He's been busy elsewhere," I told her. "Whiskey Joe's just been killed."

"It might just as easily have been me."

"I doubt it," I said. "Joe knew something about the Stanton murder and he was killed in order to hush him up. You don't know anything about anything."

"This is no time for feeble wit," she said. "I don't like this murdering business. It used to be peaceful around here. We might as well be back in the city. Anyway, I won't be left alone here any longer. Take me down to Emma's. I'm going to stay with her if you're going out again."

She got into the car. Henry told her what had taken place as I drove down to Emma's house. Emma had heard the police sirens and she was very much awake. She upbraided me roundly for leaving Joan. I drove back and picked up Smith and the redoubtable Horace.

"I knew there was something up," Smith said as we hurried along to join the captain. "Horace kept howling all evening, and he only howls when somebody dies."

"I've heard him howl lots of times," I commented skeptically.

"Yes, but this was a different howl—mournful-like. He howled that way night before last when Howard was killed. He's a smart dog. Ain't you, Horace?" he said, patting the surly beast on the head.

At first it seemed that the dog was going to be a great disappointment. There was nothing for him to smell at so he could pick up the trail of the murderer.

Smith went peering about in the underbrush with the portable light.

"Someone's been through here," he said finally. "Where's the man who went after him?"

Anderson came forward.

"I didn't go that way," he stated positively. "I went around the house."

Smith put Horace's nose on the trail. The dog sniffed at it idly and then went uncertainly forward. Finally he took up the shrill hunting cry I had heard him use when Smith and I went out after rabbits. He lunged forward, tugging at the leash. We followed with the other lights, carefully inspecting the ground as we passed. It was well covered with grass and weeds and not likely to take a good footprint impression. The trail led to a steep bank which sloped down to the edge of the brook that flowed along the Rocky Hill road. The dog stopped there and began baying eagerly, running around in an uncertain manner.

"It's no use here," Smith said quietly. "Your man's gone into the brook. We'd better try along the other bank. Maybe we can pick up the place where he came out."

He splashed across, taking the dog with him. Several hundred feet up the brook the dog took up his cry again and then stopped suddenly, yapping sharply. We came up to the spot with the lights.

"This is probably where the car was," Smith called to us. "Don't come too close. I want to get a good look before you trample the place up."

Macready stood to one side and let Smith take charge of the situation.

He searched carefully for a few minutes with the hand-light and then signaled to us to approach.

"You notice this rocky ledge?" Smith began. "Well, he probably left his car here on purpose so he wouldn't leave any tire marks. He waded up the brook to here, stepped out on the rocks, and got into his car. But he slipped up in one place. His feet were wet—the prints have dried off by now—but some of the water must have run off his leg onto this patch of dirt on the rock. One wheel of the car went right through it when he started up. The left hind one most likely, I'd say."

Smith held his light down closely over the dark spot on the rocks. The impression of an automobile tire could be seen there for a space of eighteen or twenty inches.

"I don't suppose this would help much ordinarily," Smith said apologetically. "This tire is worn smooth so you couldn't tell what kind it is. But there's something here that might be useful."

He pointed to something. There was a raised area roughly V-shaped in the dirt.

"The tread's been torn," Macready said. "We can make a plaster cast of it. It might help—if we can ever find the tire that made it. It's not much to go on, though."

"You didn't see any footprints on the way down, did you?" Henry asked.

"No, I didn't," answered Smith slowly. "None that you could make out. This feller, whoever he is, is pretty slick. He must have bound his feet with rags, because where he went into the brook there should have been some good prints in the mud. There wasn't though—just blobs that don't tell anything. It don't seem as though anything human could have a foot as shapeless as that."

We returned to the shack, leaving Smith and several of the troopers to examine the Rocky Hill road. The coroner, accompanied by Dr. Sampson, had already completed his work.

"Been dead about two hours, I'd say," the doctor told the captain briefly. "And—I don't know whether you noticed it—but this one was strangled first, too."

"Same trick all over again, eh?" Macready said.

"Signs his murders. Too bad he doesn't leave a calling card instead. Or even a print or two."

It was past midnight and there was evidently nothing more that we could do. I suggested to Henry that we go home and get some sleep.

"Okay for going back to the house," he said, "but I can't go to sleep until I get this film developed."

We said good night to Macready and Anderson and started to leave.

"I'll be over to see you in the morning," Anderson called after us.

"Sure. Join us for breakfast again," I shouted. We picked up Joan, who was very sleepy and not at all impressed by the discovery of the tire mark. Henry disappeared in the cellar with his photographic apparatus. I went to bed but I got very little rest, for Caleb Smith's dog kept howling mournfully the whole night long.

CHAPTER X
"DUST UNTO DUST RETURNETH"

The next morning I heard the sound of Anderson's motor-cycle while I was trying to get our kerosene stove lighted. Joan was still in bed; Henry was shaving and humming the *Bolero* annoyingly.

"I haven't eaten at all this morning," the trooper said cheerfully. "Since I got a regular invitation I thought I'd bring a good appetite."

"Sit down and rest your bones," I told him.

"Sitting is no treat for me," he complained. "I've got calluses the shape of a motorcycle seat now. Maybe I can help a little with the breakfast? I used to be camp cook when I was a Boy Scout."

"Well, if you want to be useful give that coffee grinder a twirl," I said, pointing to the machine that was attached to the pantry wall.

He spun it around vigorously.

"They didn't find any more tracks on the road," he volunteered.

Henry stuck a freshly shaved face through the door.

"I didn't think they would," he said brightly, "And, by the way, good morning," he called to Anderson.

"Feeling pretty chipper now, aren't you?" Anderson said. "It's fine what a little sunlight will do. You looked awful green around the gills last night."

Henry was abashed for a moment, then he began to grin. He put his hand over Anderson's big paw. The coffee in the glass under the grinder was beginning to spill over.

"Sorry," Anderson said. "I always used to grind a lot of coffee when I was in camp."

"This is no Boy Scout camp," I told him. "We hate Boy Scouts."

"Any fresh murders this morning?" Henry asked. "We city slickers expect a new one every day just to keep our jaded appetites up."

"This county's got its murder quota filled up for the next ten years right now," Anderson said grumpily. "We got our hands full already."

The trooper ate an incredible amount. When we had finished and had settled down to a quiet after-breakfast smoke over the coffee, he asked suddenly:

"Who was it that told you about this Whiskey Joe coming in to town yesterday and shooting off his mouth about the murder?"

"It was Ramsey Morgan," I said. "But that doesn't mean anything—apparently everybody in town had already heard what Whiskey Joe had been saying."

"Who else was around when you heard about it?"

I tried to recall who had been at Joe Fammel's store when we had been told the news of Whiskey Joe's visit to town.

"Well," I said rather reluctantly, "there was Joe Fammel, of course, and Fred Strong and Henry Morton. And there were a couple of men whose names I don't know."

"Morgan is that long drink of water who lives just outside the village on the South Road, isn't he?"

"That's right. First house on the left as you leave town."

"Yeah, I talked to him yesterday morning," he said, and added meditatively: "Now, he's a husky guy. He could choke a man to death. I wonder what he was doing last night between seven and ten?"

"If all the husky people around here are going to be suspected you'll have to lock half the town up."

"Well, maybe he wouldn't have to be so husky at that. What about the village idiot—the one that lives in the house you were visiting last night? I wouldn't trust a guy like that."

"Did you notice his hand?" I asked. "You can't strangle a man with only one good hand."

"Well, no. I suppose not," Anderson admitted grudgingly. "Just the same, these goofies give me the creeps. They ought to keep 'em locked up in a padded cell. You never can tell what they're going to do."

"Furthermore," I added, "Emmett Harmon was in the same room with us all last evening while we were waiting at his father's house for you to arrive. Also, he hasn't got a car."

Henry nodded confirmation.

"What about his father? He's supposed to be crippled so he can't walk. But how can we be sure of it?"

"He's paralyzed all right and I *know* he can't walk," I said. "Last winter he fell asleep with a lighted cigarette in his hand and set his bed on fire. He woke up when the bed began to burn and began to yell because he couldn't get out. Joe Fammel and a couple of men who had been hanging around the store heard him and ran into his house to save him. He was still in the burning bed when they found him. I should also like to remind you that he was in the room with us last night."

"Well, I guess that lets him out," the trooper grunted. Then a new idea hit him. "But I've heard that this fellow Fred Strong is some kind of relative of the Stantons. Maybe there's an inheritance motive somewhere. Do you know him at all?"

"Not very well," I said. "I've stopped at his place to buy gas occasionally. He's not a very friendly sort, you know. So far as I'm concerned he's no great addition to this community. It's all right with me if you find him guilty. He has a car and he doesn't live far from the Stanton house."

"Okay, I'll do my best. Now let's not get too far away from this Morgan guy. What do you know about him? He has a car all right."

"Nearly everybody has a car around here. I have one myself."

"What do you know about Morgan?" Anderson insisted.

"Not very much," I admitted. "He seems to be a decent sort. Plain farmer, born and lived here all his life. I never heard of any trouble between him and Stanton."

"Impossible," murmured Henry. "You're spoiling Stanton's record."

"Well, maybe there was some trouble," I said testily. "I don't know. I haven't been keeping a record of Howard Stanton's quarrels."

"Sure, I know how you feel about it," put in Anderson sympathetically. "Morgan has a married son who lives in the little house in back of his father's place, hasn't he?"

I nodded.

Anderson leaned back in his chair.

"There's too damned many people around here who might have killed Stanton—and Whiskey Joe, too," he added. "It's going to be a lot of fun getting alibis from a town full of people."

"How about establishing a really good motive?" suggested Henry. "Maybe you could work from that."

"Good motive, hell!" snorted Anderson. "I knew a case where a man was killed for a dime in a crap game. The motive doesn't have to be good. People do lots of funny things."

"You know," began Henry, "the more I think about the bit of tire track that was found on the road last night the less I think of it as evidence."

"Sure. It's lousy evidence. Just because someone was parked on that road last night doesn't mean we can pin the murder on him. It might have been a couple out necking. Someone might have borrowed the car. Maybe somebody put the tire track there just for a plant. You're right. It's lousy evidence. But it's all the evidence we have, and I'd like to find the tire that has that particular cut in it." He sighed. "We'd at least have somebody to talk to," he added pathetically.

"Do you suppose I could get one of the plaster casts?" inquired Henry. "I'd make it my business to examine a lot of tires around here. It might help some."

"Oh, I suppose it might be arranged," Anderson said idly. "They'll probably make up a whole slew of casts from it. I'll try to get you one."

"Thanks," said Henry gratefully. "Don't forget."

Anderson got up and stretched himself sleepily.

"I'm going to run down to headquarters and get a snooze. I've been up all night watching Whiskey Joe's shack so nobody could steal it. Are you gents going to the Stanton funeral? It's going to be held this afternoon."

"We'll be there all right, if they'll let us in," Henry promised. He went outside with the trooper and the two of them went into a conversation that lasted for a long time.

The funeral of Howard Stanton was extraordinarily well attended. It was the custom in Brookdale to keep open house at a funeral. Ordinarily everyone was welcome. But at the Stanton funeral the crowd was so big that only those who could prove some acquaintance with the deceased were admitted inside the white fence that surrounded the house. Arthur Fammel, father of the store-keeper, was guarding the gate. He knew me, and after a brief discussion of the second murder, he permitted us to pass through the gate.

Joan came with us. Women and priests, I have noted, have a natural affinity for life's more serious functions—birth, marriage, and death. Most men naturally feel awkward and out of place at such times.

This was exemplified at the funeral. The women crowded readily into the house; the men hung back and gathered in little knots under the maple trees that shaded the lawn. There they talked of crops and the weather; in fact of any subject under the sun except the dead man and his burial.

The undertaker, looking very solemn in his black frock coat, came over to us.

"If you wish to view the body now, please pass into the parlor," he said in a voice that reminded me of greasy dishwater.

He opened the screen door invitingly.

Stanton was lying in an elaborate casket. The silk lining of the coffin had been piled up skillfully around his head. His peaceful countenance was a triumph of mortuary art. Henry stared at him solemnly.

There were only a few people in the parlor where the coffin was placed. I recognized Dr. Allen Stanton, Howard's brother, among them. The physician who had assisted the coroner was sitting next to him. Huddled in a far corner of the room were the Strongs, relatives of the Stantons through the marriage of the doctor, whose wife, however, had been dead for many years. George Hathaway and Mrs. Denner were standing humbly in the hall outside the parlor.

The undertaker permitted us only a brief glance at the body. Then he hurried us outside.

"The house is pretty full," he whispered with satisfaction. "You can go upstairs—there's a lot of people up there already. Or you can go out to the kitchen where it isn't so crowded."

We chose the kitchen. A dozen people were seated there on uncomfortable folding chairs. From where I sat I could see into the dining room. It was crowded with people—the whole house was evidently packed with living, breathing humanity, but no one made a sound.

We waited in that silent house for at least twenty minutes. Then the minister, whom we could not see, suddenly began to speak:

"Let us begin this service with a reading from the Scriptures: *The Lord is my shepherd . . . the valley . . . of the shadow of death . . . my cup runneth over. . . .*"

The beautiful words flowed on meaninglessly. Outside, the men on the lawn were still talking of mundane things. Beyond them the crowd behind the fence kept up a steady murmur. There was a short prayer. Then the thin voices of the choir broke out into a hymn. They sang abominably.

The meeting broke up finally. We went out on the kitchen porch. Six neighbors were carrying the heavy casket across the lawn. Under the green shade of the maples they passed, bearing the murdered body of Howard Stanton from the house of his fathers. The crowd followed. The sound of conversation grew louder. The funeral coach moved slowly down the driveway toward the road, followed by a dozen automobiles. Then the procession turned southward over the dusty roads to Whitechurch where the Stanton family had a vault in the churchyard.

CHAPTER XI
WE DISCUSS ONE OF THE FINE ARTS

The crowd broke up quickly. Everyone even remotely connected with the Stanton family had gone in the funeral procession to Whitechurch. A few neighbors stayed to clean up and put the house to rights but in a few minutes the green lawn was almost deserted. We walked slowly toward our car.

"Do you think the murderer was there?" Joan asked.

Henry shrugged his shoulders. "My guess is that he was," he said slowly. "If he was crazy enough to treat Stanton's dead body the way he did, he might just be crazy enough to attend the funeral."

Caleb Smith was standing idly by the gate as we passed through. I invited him to ride back with us.

"That's certainly a better funeral than Joe is going to get," he said bitterly. "Potter's field—that's where he'll go. He didn't have a cent to leave to the undertaker."

"Why don't you take up a subscription?" Henry suggested. "I'll gladly chip in."

Joan and I offered to contribute also.

"I suppose Doctor Stanton will take over the house now," I ventured.

"Most likely," Smith said. "He can carry on his doctoring business here just as well as at Baileystown and this is a better house than the one he's living in now. He's pretty well fixed though, I guess. When he heard about his brother's death—he was out in Cleveland at some kind of doctors' meeting when it happened—he hired an airplane and flew back in three hours. That takes money."

Airplanes, of course, were a great luxury to the simple folk of Brookdale, although the town was on a mail route with airplanes passing over all day and all night long.

Henry settled down with a sigh into one of the deck chairs on our porch.

"The trouble with a murder in real life," he said, "is that you get just so far and then you stop. In a mystery story the author is always thoughtful enough to provide plenty of clues. Now what have the police actually found out about the murder of Howard Stanton? Very little indeed. They know that someone waded up the brook, strangled him, pounded his head in with a rock, went through the formality of hanging him to a tree, took care not to leave a single fingerprint or foot-track, and then disappeared. So what?" He sighed and continued. "Then Whiskey Joe, who might have given the cops a tip, was bumped off in exactly the same way. This time they learned that the murderer uses an automobile and that one of his tires—on the left-hand side and probably the rear one—has a V-shaped stone cut. If he's really smart he'll change the tires and destroy the old ones. Everybody around here has a car. Every car has at least four tires. Anybody might have done the actual killing. No wonder so many murders go unsolved. The murderers are so damned unsportsmanlike!"

"You're spoiled," I said. "You've been reading too many mystery stories and you have developed a mystery-story attitude toward the case. You're too sure that the solution is going to be worked out in the back of the book and you're just trying to beat the author to it. Now that you are confronted with a real murder which might have been committed by any one of a hundred people you're stumped because there are no jeweled daggers, poisoned darts, or pseudo-scientific mechanisms that were used to do the actual slaying. You'd better leave this case to the police and stick to cotton converting and the lending library. The police at least are making a careful check of all the alibis and they may turn up something yet."

Henry looked at me quizzically. "And just what, if I may be permitted to ask, have the police accomplished?"

"Well, their method takes time. You know that. They have to do a lot of questioning, and trace down all sorts of trivial clues, conflicting alibis, and such. But I'd back their traditional methods against any intuitional flash of detective genius from Philo Vance to Lord Peter Wimsey."

"So you *have* been reading mystery stories!" he exclaimed triumphantly.

"Not at all," I said scornfully. "I never read one in my life. I just happened to glance through a critical article on the genre in *The Saturday Review of Literature.*"

"That's the first step," he said. "We'll get you yet. Would you like to read—?"

"No, I wouldn't. I've got work enough of my own to do. There's more fun turning up an unknown species of slime mold than there is in taking refuge in the sort of escape literature you're addicted to. Besides it's more useful."

"Useful? What's useful about it? You know perfectly well that the Myxomycetes are quite harmless—except that one causes clubroot of cabbage and I haven't seen you work out any bright discoveries for preventing that."

"That's agricultural-school stuff," I protested. "I'm working in the field of pure research."

"The very essence of uselessness, I'd say. It's too bad we haven't got any evidence like the mildew Poe introduced into *The Mystery of Marie Rogêt.* You might be able to do some really constructive work in this case if we had."

"What kind of mildew was it?" I asked with some interest.

"Do you mean to say you've never even read Poe?"

"Certainly I've read Poe. What's the story about the mildew?"

Henry grinned. "I've got *The Omnibus of Crime* with me. I'll lend it to you. It has the Marie Rogêt story in it and the introduction by Dorothy Sayers might do you some good, too. I'll run upstairs and get it."

"Don't bother. Some other time. I can't get started on that sort of thing now. I ought to be out in the laboratory working."

Henry looked disappointed.

"Well, I think I'll go and print the negative I made of Whiskey Joe's body," he said. "It certainly must be dry by now."

He had told me the first thing in the morning that he had obtained a fairly good negative after intensifying it twice.

I tossed my cigarette away and stood up.

"Has Anderson told you anything about what the police have accomplished in checking alibis?" I ventured idly.

"Yes, he has. I got it out of him this morning. They've found out that most of these farm people were right at home Tuesday night. If any one of them is actually guilty the whole family would swear, of course, that the guilty person was in the house all evening. And he might even have sneaked out without their knowledge. It's very disappointing.

"And so far as motive is concerned we don't get anywhere either. Everybody hated Stanton, but nobody hated him enough to have a genuinely good reason to kill him. At least not that we know of. The only person who stood to profit by his death was his brother. And he was in Cleveland at the time of the murder."

"How about George Hathaway? What have the police been doing about him?"

"They've been thinking about him plenty. Anderson told me he would probably have been arrested this morning on suspicion if it hadn't been for something that happened last night during the killing of Whiskey Joe. Anderson stopped at the Stanton house on the way back from his wild goose chase. He found that a trooper had been detailed to stay there, and he had been in the kitchen playing checkers with Hathaway all evening. Pretty good alibi, eh?"

"It'll do," I admitted. "Why didn't you tell me about it?"

"Oh, it didn't seem important. I just crossed Hathaway off the list of suspects. And anyway, I thought you weren't interested in this case."

"I'm not. It's just that there isn't anything else to talk to you about."

"You're a fine one to say that!" he said indignantly. "The only thing you were ever interested in is a lot of slimy fungus with Latin names that no one else ever heard of. When you come up against a problem that concerns human beings you're like a child and you try to act superior by scoffing at it."

"All right. All right. Keep your shirt on," I said soothingly. "Let's stick to the subject since you think it's such an important one. We were talking about possible suspects, I believe. Now how about Whiskey Joe himself? He might very well have killed Stanton. He was certainly near the scene of the crime at the right time and full of liquor too."

"Mm," said Henry thoughtfully. "And then somebody else killed Joe. Possible. Possible enough. Very clever, in fact. But even if it's true we still have to find out who killed Joe. Of course, it doesn't fit in with my own ideas about the crime but there might be something in your theory anyway. I'm still open-minded."

He fell silent and looked out over the valley.

"Brookdale is a swell place to stage a murder in, all right," he said finally. "All this country to make a getaway in. I always thought it was a cinch to pull off a successful murder in the city. There are so many people you can lose yourself among. I begin to see certain advantages in this rural atmosphere though. It's so nice and restful."

CHAPTER XII
SYMBOLS OF MURDER

I worked at my book until late in the afternoon. When I entered the house I found that Henry had begun to display a sudden interest in Emma. He was sitting in the kitchen while she was preparing dinner and he was talking to her in low tones. From scraps of conversation that I overheard I gathered that he was pumping her for information about the local townspeople. Evidently flattered by his attention, she made an elaborate chocolate cake—Henry's favorite dessert. After dinner, while I was driving her to her home, she remarked several times what an extraordinarily nice person Henry was—and so smart! As she was getting out of the car she simpered:

"Mr. Henry has a surprise for you. I'll let him tell you about it himself."

I drove back quickly to the house.

"Have you been trying to propose to Emma?" I demanded accusingly of Henry.

Joan giggled.

"Don't be silly," said Henry turning red. "What did she say?"

"She said you had a surprise for us, and after the way you've been wooing her all afternoon I'm prepared for anything. What's the surprise?"

Henry drew out a cigarette and lighted it with great deliberation.

"I've decided that I might as well take my vacation now instead of later in the summer, and I'm going to spend it here in Brookdale. I asked Emma to put me up. She doesn't take boarders ordinarily, but she's making an exception in my case—due to my unusual charm, I believe."

"That's absurd," protested Joan. "Not your charm, of course," she said quickly. "But you can easily stay here. We've got lots of room and we were going to ask you to stay with us for your vacation anyway, weren't we, Jim?"

"No," I said. "We were not. But stay here anyhow."

"Nice of you, but I couldn't think of it," Henry said. "While I haven't imposed on you nearly enough, I really do want to see the rural American in his natural habitat. I want to go to the people, live with them, be one of them!" He flung his arms wide and struck an attitude. "I also want to take a vacation," he added, yawning.

"Aren't you going back to your office—ever?" said Joan.

"Yes, I'll have to report back on Monday to prepare the boss for the shock of getting along without me for two weeks, but I guess I can get back here on Tuesday evening. By the way, you won't mind picking me up at the train, will you?"

"I will mind," I grumbled, "but I'll do it. Tell me, what pearls of wisdom did you garner from Emma during your conversation this afternoon?"

"Nothing terribly pertinent, but a lot of interesting odds and ends. Do you know, for instance, why Whiskey Joe was called Whiskey?"

"Because he drank so much of it, I suppose."

"Wrong as usual," said Henry calmly. "And you ought to be ashamed of yourself. Living here for nearly five years and not knowing how one of your most distinguished citizens got his name! Whiskey Joe never touched a drop of whiskey in his life. He drank apple brandy, vulgarly but incorrectly known as apple whiskey. Also called apple, applejack, in France Calvados, *eau de vie de marc de cidre,* or what have you? However, he wasn't called Whiskey just because he drank the stuff. He once actually owned a cider mill and distillery. You can see the ruins of the place on the Calverton road a few miles from here. His propensity for sampling his own wares, and the end of that great experiment in morals, Prohibition, finally brought him to his recent low estate. *Requiescat in pace!*"

"That reminds me," Joan said, jumping up. "We have some apple whiskey. Shall I mix a drink?"

"Apple brandy," breathed Henry reprovingly. "But it's a good idea anyway. It makes a swell drink no matter what you call it."

I helped Joan squeeze the lemons.

"Maybe it's a good thing Henry will be here next week," she said thoughtfully. "He can entertain Helen. She probably will be plenty bored after working on your old herbarium files all day long."

"What's that?" Henry asked, overhearing us.

"There's going to be a charming young lady out here to help Jim. Tell Henry all about her," she instructed me demurely, her matchmaking instinct coming to the fore.

"Well," I began dutifully, "she's a graduate student who has specialized in the Myxomycetes under my guidance."

"Go on," said Henry shuddering. "I hate her already. A decayed-wood-and-dead-leaves grubber spending her youth glaring through bespectacled eyes into a microscope at ugly little toadstools. Go on. Tell me the worst."

"She doesn't wear glasses, and Myxomycetes are not toadstools," I corrected. "They are microscopic slime molds—"

"Yes, yes," he said. "I've heard you explain all that before. I've always thought it a pity that a bright young man like you should waste the best years of his life on baby toadstools, but now you have gone and seduced a young girl—" "Oh, Jim! Again?" Joan said sorrowfully.

"Seduced a young girl from the normal interests of her sex and age," Henry went on implacably, "and encouraged her to take up the Myxomycetes as a career. She must have done it through desperation, though, I suppose. I can just see her." He closed his eyes and accompanied his description with gestures. "Flat-chested, thick-ankled, near-sighted, nasal-voiced and—shall we say—a bit hermaphroditic? You know, the tailor-suited kind."

Joan giggled. "That's a perfect description of Helen. As a matter of fact her twin sister is a dancer in the Vanities. Helen is even better-looking. Also, she's a blonde. However, if the young lady's intellectual accomplishments frighten you, I dare say she can find other company. It's only an hour's drive out here from the college, and I'm sure that there are some young men there for the summer session who would be willing to travel for sixty minutes to visit her."

"Wait a minute," Henry said, sitting up and addressing me. "Is that true about her sister being a Vanities girl?"

I nodded. "Yes, but I doubt whether Helen would be interested in you. She isn't the chorus-girl type at all. She's much too refined and serious-minded for a young wastrel like you. She's a brilliant young graduate student who will be a Ph.D. next year, and she probably wouldn't care for cotton converting."

"If she can stand the Myxomycetes she'll think cotton converting is one gay, mad whirl," muttered Henry. "When is she coming out here?"

"Tuesday evening," said Joan promptly. "I thought you might meet her in the city and help her with her luggage. But, of course, if you aren't interested—"

"She lives in New York?"

"Mm. With her sister."

"Well, now I suppose I ought to be polite," Henry said grudgingly. "What part of town does she live in?"

"On Bank Street. Only a couple of blocks from you."

"What's her name?"

"Helen Douglas."

"Is her sister's name Marjorie Douglas?"

"That's right," Joan said. "You may have seen Marjorie's picture in the rotogravure section of the *Times* a few Sundays ago."

"Oh, yes," breathed Henry. "I did. And you say Helen is even better-looking—and blonde? Why it would be downright rude not to help her to the station since she lives so near to me. We could talk about the dear little Myxomycetes on the train. You know, I always did think there must be a certain fascination about slime molds if they could interest people of your intellectual caliber. Have you?—"

And then suddenly the lights went out and we were plunged into absolute darkness.

"The fuse must have blown," Joan said nervously.

"Henry, have you got a match? I don't seem to have one," I said, fumbling in my pockets.

"I'm trying to find one," he said. "I left a pack on the table here. Damn!"

Joan seized my arm and dug her fingers into it.

"There's someone in the kitchen," she said in a tense voice.

I sat still for a moment listening. I heard a floor board creak. Then I felt a draught of fresh air sweep through the house. Henry struck a match. It sputtered and was promptly blown out.

"Don't do that," I whispered. "If you make a light he can see us in here. He's gone outside. The kitchen door is open. That's why there's a draught."

"Where's your shotgun?" Henry asked in a voice that he tried to make sound casual.

"Upstairs, locked up in a closet. Come on, let's have a try at him anyway."

We rushed into the kitchen. The door leading out to the road was standing wide open. I went out on the porch followed closely by Henry and Joan. It was very dark. The sky was overcast and it was impossible to see any distance at all.

"Sh—" Joan warned. "Down by the brook. Do you hear it?"

I heard a slight crackling sound.

"We can't go chasing through the woods in this darkness," I said. "I'll get my searchlight out of the car."

"Shall we go after him?" I asked Henry, when I had turned on the cheerful ray of light.

He shook his head. "I don't think it's any use now. He's got too much of a start. Let's have a look at the house and see what he wanted there. You'd better go down in the cellar and see what's wrong with the lights first."

We all went, using the outside cellar entrance. I flashed my light on the central switchboard. The master switch had been pulled. I pushed it back into place again and I could see the light stream out of the living-room windows overhead.

We went up the cellar stairs and I noticed that the door at the top leading into the kitchen was open. I pulled on the kitchen light.

"Here's something," said Henry pointing to a table that stood against the wall.

A crumpled bit of white paper had been hurriedly spread out there. There was something written on it in crudely drawn capital letters. I bent over to read the message:

KEEP YOUR NOSE OUT OF THIS

On the paper two small objects were lying—a white pebble and a short bit of string.

"Don't touch anything," Henry warned me. "There may be fingerprints."

Joan was looking curiously at the pebble and the string.

"What do you suppose those things are there for?"

"It's pretty obvious, isn't it?" said Henry unkindly, "when you think how both Stanton and Whiskey Joe were—"

Joan looked at us with a white face. "You don't suppose it could be a joke?" she asked miserably.

We went back into the living room for a brief deliberation.

"I haven't the heart to phone Anderson," Henry said.
"He didn't get any sleep last night. I suppose the fingerprints—if there are any—can wait until morning."

"We oughtn't to leave the paper lying around down
here though."

"You're right. We'd better put it away in some safe
place."

He shoved a piece of cardboard under the message
and carried it upstairs and put it in the top drawer of his
bureau.

"I don't like this!" Joan wailed. "Lock the house up
tight and put the shotgun in our bedroom." She stopped
suddenly. "Say, where was Tinkel when all this was hap-
pening? She might at least have barked."

"That's an idea," Henry said. "Where is she now, as a
matter of fact?"

I went back into the living room and stuck my flashlight under the couch. It was one of Tinkel's favorite re-
tiring places. She was there all right, snoozing peacefully.
She opened one eye lazily, and yawned. Then she crawled
out and turned over on her back, begging us to scratch her
belly.

"That's a swell watchdog you have," jeered Henry.

"She's not supposed to be a watchdog," Joan said, taking the dog in her arms. "Besides, she isn't feeling well
now."

Tinkel licked her face gratefully.

CHAPTER XIII
THE EXPERTS TAKE A HAND

I was awakened at an early hour by loud and disagreeable noises. I got up and looked out of the window. Henry was bathing in the brook and he was singing at the top of his voice as he splashed around in the water. Tinkel was barking an accompaniment. I drew on a bathrobe and ran down to the pool.

Henry greeted me cheerfully. "I couldn't sleep. I lay awake trying to figure this whole thing out. I'm happy to announce that the clear light of reason is beginning to dawn. Last night's visit started me off on a new track that I think is going to lead somewhere. I'm sure there won't be any fingerprints on that note, but I have an idea how it got there."

"Well, how did it?"

"Did it what?"

"Get there, you idiot!"

"Oh, yes, get there. Well, I don't think I ought to talk about it yet. First of all I have only a suspicion. And secondly, it just isn't done. Detectives never tell at this stage of the game."

I stepped gingerly into the cold water.

"You're not going to pull that mystery stuff with me, I hope. Why, you wouldn't have had the chance to be in on this murder case if I, out of the goodness of my heart, hadn't—" My foot slipped on a stone and I suddenly sat down in the brook.

Henry laughed unfeelingly.

"Well, how about it?" I asked again, gasping.

He shook his head. "Certainly not. It's not considered good form for a detective to reveal anything until he has an open and shut case against the murderer."

"And that, I'd say, was a practice that has probably saved a lot of detectives from making damned fools of themselves."

"You're absolutely right," he said climbing out and starting to rub himself vigorously with a bath towel. "You know the old saying about not showing a half-finished job to a—"

"To hell with you and your mysteries and your old sayings. I'm still betting on the police."

"Okay. But don't forget they're getting a lot of assistance from me."

"Nice of you."

"Oh, I'm very public-spirited. Hadn't you noticed?"

I dove under the water and swam along the bottom. It was very cool and strange there. I stayed under as long as I could. Henry was very annoying at times. When I emerged he was putting on his bathrobe.

"I'd like to borrow your car," he said. "I want to run down to the village to phone Anderson."

"Go ahead," I said ungraciously. "But pick up Emma on the way back. And for the love of Mike don't tell her anything about last night's visitor or we'll have to get another cook!"

I dried myself leisurely and went back to the house. I lit the stove, mopped up the kitchen and started breakfast. Joan came down, yawning, and went to the brook to bathe.

By the time the bacon was beginning to smell good, Joan, Henry, and Emma arrived—almost simultaneously.

"Did you get Anderson?" I asked Henry.

He nodded briefly. "He'll be here in an hour. I have it all arranged."

"He's going to miss breakfast. It won't seem quite the same without him."

Emma insisted on being heard.

"Mr. Henry tells me he told you," she began.

"About his staying with you during his vacation, you mean?" Joan interrupted. "Well, I'm sure he'll get some good country cooking."

"That he will," Emma said firmly. "And I've promised to get him a pint of cream every morning."

Cream was an unprecedented luxury in Brookdale, used only by summer residents and transplanted city folks like ourselves. Condensed milk had driven it off the tables even of those who owned cows.

"I'm sure he'll enjoy his stay with you," said Joan, visibly impressed. "Emma, will you clean the house especially well today? Some people may drop in this evening."

"Who's coming?" I asked curiously as Emma went out on the porch to set the breakfast table.

"No one that I know of. I just said that so she'd clean up decently."

"That's fine," I said. "Then we can get some more work done tonight. This confounded inquest is going to kill most of the day, I'm afraid."

Joan pouted. "I thought we might go to the movies."

"You go with Henry," I told her. "I've got to get that damned book moving along faster. I've got only six weeks to finish the research now."

"Oh, you and your confounded book!" said Joan.

"My confounded book will keep you in calories," I observed sagely. "And you've got to finish the drawing you started yesterday."

Anderson arrived in a Ford coupe with Hamilton, the plain-clothes man we had met on the night Whiskey Joe had been killed. Henry told them about our mysterious visitor and he produced the note as evidence.

"I've been hoping that it might be someone's stupid idea of a practical joke," Joan said to Hamilton.

"It would be a pretty lousy joke, all right," he agreed. "I hope you're right though. But we'll try the paper for fingerprints. Maybe someone was careless."

He took out a kit bag and removed a bottle of powder which he spread lightly over the paper. It revealed only a few shapeless smudges. He turned the paper over and tried again with the same lack of results. He even tried the pebble.

"Fingerprint evidence," he said sadly, "is rapidly becoming obsolete. Its usefulness has been spoiled for us by a lot of mystery-story writers and yellow journalists. I can take this paper to the police laboratory and try it with silver nitrate for latent fingerprints, but I don't think it will show any. I'm convinced that the paper was handled only by gloved hands."

"How about tracing the origin of the paper itself—or the handwriting?" Henry suggested.

"The paper is common white wrapping paper of the country-store variety. It probably came from the local store here and anyone who is a customer—which means anyone around here, since there's only one store—might have had such a piece of paper in his house. I'll take a look at the wrapping paper at Fammel's on the chance that this paper might not have come from there, but it's my guess right now that it has."

"And the writing?"

"Made with a medium soft pencil and from the inclination of the very badly drawn letters I'd say that it was made by the left hand of a person who is normally right-handed. No misspellings."

"There wasn't much chance to spell anything incorrectly," Henry pointed out. "They're all common words and the longest has only four letters."

"I suspect that whoever was responsible for this message had all that figured out. The question is—are you going to take his advice? I think you ought to. This is a police affair. You're only putting your neck out inviting trouble and I think this fellow means business. Remember that he killed Joe Hartram simply because he was afraid he might talk."

Henry looked thoughtful.

"I think you ought to go back to the city," I advised him seriously. "Come out later in the summer, if you want to, and spend your vacation here when the whole business has blown over."

"That's right," said Hamilton. "Very sensible advice. We've got enough to do already without having to offer police protection to amateurs."

Henry flushed.

"I'll think about it," he said. "Don't forget that I'm a witness in this case though. I've already been asked to attend the inquest this afternoon."

The two policemen drove off then and left us with several hours on our hands before the inquest was due to start. I invited Henry to get a little exercise by helping me weed the garden. One of the things I have discovered after several years of living in the country is that city visitors, no matter how ardent they wax over the joys of gardening in prospect, become strangely reluctant to work in a garden when actually given the chance. In fact, only one, out of all the guests we have had at our house, has ever pitched in and done some serious weeding. And that one, needless to say, was not Henry. He got out of it quite neatly by pleading the necessity of doing a little morning sleuthing.

"By the way," I said to him as he climbed into the car, "you forgot to make a photographic copy of the message before the police impounded it as evidence."

"Don't be foolish," he said, stepping on the starter. "I shot a flock of negatives of it last night before I went to bed."

He started to turn Little Bertha around. Then he stopped and asked suddenly: "You've got a pair of trout-fishing boots, haven't you?"

"Yes, but the season is over."

"I have no intention of going after trout," he said. "But I'd like to borrow your boots for a little brook fishing of another kind."

CHAPTER XIV
HENRY CATCHES A STRANGE FISH

About an hour later I heard Henry drive up. He dashed in and dropped into the chair beside my desk. Joan raised her eyes from the microscope and turned around curiously.

"Well," he began, "I think I've found something."

I waited for him to go on.

"You remember what Cal Smith said about the murderer binding his feet in rags so as to leave no footprints? Well, I used your trout-fishing boots to go wading in the brook along the Rocky Hill road. On the bottom, near the spot where we saw the tire track, I found this wedged in between two stones," Triumphantly he laid a tiny scrap of wet burlap in front of me.

I picked it up and looked at it casually.

"You see that blue stuff on it?" Henry pointed eagerly. "That's part of the printing on a burlap bag. It might be possible to trace the bag through it. Now you have pigment and burlap to work on. You're supposed to be a scientist, let's see you do your stuff."

"I'm no Craig Kennedy," I said irritably.

"Let me have it, Henry," said Joan, and pointed at me sternly. "God there is in a tantrum this morning because his damned old book isn't going fast enough to suit him and he resents the time he's going to have to spend at the inquest. He deplores these trivial interruptions that stop the mighty progress of the immortal Myxomycetes."

I pushed my manuscript away with a sigh of resignation. "Let me have your filthy rag and if there is anything to find out about it, I'll find it."

I caught Joan winking at Henry and they both tiptoed outside with exaggerated solicitude to smoke cigarettes. I slipped the piece of burlap under a low-powered microscope which told me nothing. Then I examined it carefully without any lenses at all.

A few minutes later I walked out into the sunlight, sat down beside them, and lit my pipe.

"Well, what did you find?" Henry asked jauntily.

"Nothing that any literate adult with an I.Q. of more than 37 couldn't see at first glance. The blue stuff is ink right enough. If you wish, I can send some of the pigment to the college laboratory and have an exact analysis made. But it's hardly necessary. Take a good look at the shape of the ink impressions. I assume that you know the letters of the alphabet."

I spread the tiny scrap out on my knee.

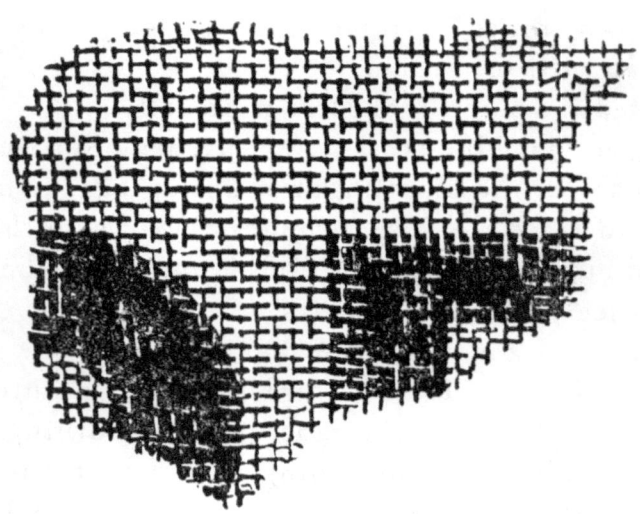

"These are pieces of large letters—probably the trade name of the product packed in the bag." I took out a pencil and wrote the letters of the alphabet in capitals.

ABCDEFGHIJKLMNOPQRSTUVWXYZ

"Now from the shape of the upper right corner, the first letter must be B, P, or R. The second letter must be an E or an F. I'd suggest that you take the car and run down to the mill at Calverton. Ask for Hank Alpaugh. He'll let you take a look at the various kinds of feed, flour, and such stuff. Try to find one printed in blue with these letters occurring next to each other. And you didn't need a laboratory to find all this out."

"Righto," said Henry, patting me on the shoulder approvingly. "I'd have gotten around to it. But it seemed a shame to let all those swell microscopes go to waste, and I wanted to give you a chance to turn your powerful intellect on the problem."

"Make it snappy," I said. "We've got to have some lunch and be at that damned inquest at two o'clock."

Henry returned a short while later enthusiastically waving a burlap sack.

"EUREKA!" he shouted. "I've found it all right. *Eureka* is so appropriate, too."

"Why?" asked Joan.

"Eureka is a brand name," he said showing us the bag. "Note the juxtaposition of the R and E. The blue ink, the size of the letters, and the kind of burlap all check. It's Eureka sure enough. And now get this:

"Eureka is the brand name for a very special kind of chicken feed. Your friend, Mr. Alpaugh, explained to me just what it is used for but that doesn't matter. What does count is this: Eureka is a brand he doesn't ordinarily stock. Last fall he got five hundred pounds of it on special order for—well, who do you think?"

"Mahatma Gandhi," ventured Joan.

"How many guesses do we get?" I asked.

"This is no laughing matter," said Henry. "This bit of burlap may help to send someone to the electric chair."

"Well, go on," I said soberly. "Who ordered it?"

"Howard Stanton!"

"Stanton!"

Henry nodded. "The feed was doubtless used up during the winter and the empty bags were probably left around somewhere in his barn. Whoever killed Whiskey Joe must have had easy access to the Stanton barn."

"Wait a minute," Joan said. "Bags don't always stay put. Stanton might have used them to pack potatoes or some such stuff. Somebody could have bought the potatoes—and the bags. How did the mill happen to have that one on hand if it was a brand bought only on special order?"

"It was a sample," Henry said. "I bought it, and had them empty the feed out."

Joan looked skeptical. "It all sounds pretty farfetched to me."

"Don't be so damned encouraging," Henry said, carefully folding up the bag.

I looked at my watch. "We'd better get lunch over with in a hurry if we're going to make that inquest," I warned him.

"All right," he said cheerfully, "I want to see Anderson as soon as possible so I can talk to him about tracing the Eureka bags. Maybe he'll think they're worth something as a clue. Meanwhile I'm going to make a photograph of this piece of burlap before I turn it over to the police."

Except for the changed faces in the jury, the second inquest was a curious repetition of the first. It was held in the same place, the same crowd was there, and, of course, the same coroner presided.

When we entered, Henry spotted Anderson in the hallway leading to the meeting room and immediately went into a whispered colloquy with him. I saw Henry show him the bit of burlap he had found in the brook.

Henry joined us inside and told us that Anderson had seemed quite impressed by his discovery and had advised him to withhold this new evidence for the benefit of the police. He said that the police had also arranged to suppress the evidence of the tire track left on Rocky Hill road. If the murderer had not already removed the incriminating tire from his car there was no use in giving him a public warning to do so.

Anderson was the first witness called. He described how Henry had summoned him by telephone; how we had gone to the dwelling of one Joseph Hartram to get information regarding the Stanton murder and how we had found that Hartram had been murdered in his bed.

He went on to relate how he had thought he heard someone leave the house as we approached, and he described in detail—with the assistance of a county map provided by the coroner—the exact route he had taken in pursuit of the car.

Joe Fammel and Ramsey Morgan were called to make formal identification of the body. The coroner questioned them further as to what Whiskey Joe had said on his ill-fated visit to the town that afternoon. They repeated, with some disagreement as to the exact wording, what they had already told us.

Henry was the next witness, and the coroner immediately set out to discover whether Henry had known the deceased. It seemed absurd to try to implicate Henry in the murder since he had no possible motive. Furthermore, he would surely be absolved by the medical evidence which would naturally make it clear that Whiskey Joe had been killed only a few minutes before we discovered his body, but I have already expressed my opinion of the coroner's sagacity.

Henry, I must say, bore up very well under questioning. After the coroner had exhausted every possibility Henry asked if he might speak for a moment on something that he thought was pertinent to the case. Permission was granted, somewhat ungraciously.

"I should like to tell the court," Henry said, "about my own interest in this case. I was invited to come out here by Mr. James Whitby, a resident of this community. As you know, Mr. Whitby was present at the finding of the murdered corpse of Howard Stanton. Although no possible suspicion could be cast on him he naturally was in a very unpleasant position. He called on me to assist him. I am not what you would call a detective—I have no professional interest of any kind in this case. Nevertheless I do possess some elementary knowledge of criminology, particularly that part of it which has to do with murder. I know that the police have been making a very thorough investigation of this affair and I have no doubt that they will succeed in solving the case. I have simply been trying to supplement their activities in my own small way."

Henry bowed to the coroner and was permitted to return to his seat.

"You've got a hell of a nerve," I whispered to him as he sat down. "Called on you to assist me! Where do you get that stuff? Besides, you sounded like a very weak imitation of every story-book detective I ever heard about."

"That," said Henry firmly, "is exactly how I wanted to sound. Nobody will take me seriously after hearing a speech like that—least of all the murderer."

I heard the coroner calling my name and I stepped forward.

After a brief inquiry into the actual finding of the body the coroner again tried to find out whether Henry could have been implicated in any way. I was irritated by this senseless questioning. After all, Henry was my guest. I burst out in his defense.

"Mr. Hale has already explained to you that he is greatly interested in the subject of murder. His interest, of course, is a purely impersonal one. I may say that it has already exposed him to some risk. Last night our house was entered by some unknown person who shut off the lights at the master switch and then left a message on our kitchen table warning Mr. Hale to keep out of this affair."

Henry was motioning to me and there was a murmur of conversation in the room. The coroner rapped on the table for order.

"And this message—where is it now?" the coroner asked.

"It was turned over to the police this morning."

I was permitted to return to my seat. Henry glared at me as I sat down.

"You shouldn't have said that," he whispered. "I'm trying to make myself look like an idiot. Idiots don't get warnings."

The next witness was Hamilton. In order to satisfy public curiosity he first read the warning message, described how he had examined it fruitlessly for fingerprints, and hurriedly passed on to other evidence directly pertaining to the murder. He didn't mention the pebble and string at all.

He described the condition of Whiskey Joe's body and then brought out that the dead man had had on his person the sum of $4.19 in cash and a check for $6 dated two days before the murder, made out to "Cash" and signed by Howard Stanton. The court buzzed again, but all that I could see that it meant was that Stanton had probably purchased a gallon of applejack and given Joe a check in payment. (Six dollars was the current quotation.) The fact that Stanton and Whiskey Joe had quarreled in the past would not necessarily have affected their business relationship.

Hamilton also presented for the benefit of the court the actual stone with which the murder of Whiskey Joe had been committed, and he pointed out certain smudges on its blood-stained surface which he said had been made by gloved fingers. The gloves appeared to be of smooth leather, and, unfortunately the marks they had left were too indistinct to have any identification value. From the size and position of the markings, however, he ventured to express an opinion that the hands which had made them were fairly large ones. The stone had been picked up by the murderer from a wall just outside the door of the shack. He also produced as evidence the blood-stained rope that had been around the murdered man's neck. The rope, he said, had belonged to Whiskey Joe. The murderer had found it in the shack and had probably intended to hang the corpse from the rafters but he had been frightened away before he could do so.

He went on to describe the condition of the room which had showed no signs of a struggle, indicating that the occupant had still been unconscious when the murderer had committed his crime.

Hamilton made way for Caleb Smith who told of his successful attempt to follow the murderer's trail to the spot where he had left his car. He brought out the fact that the unknown assassin had probably bound his feet with rags, since the impressions in the soft mud at the edge of the brook were shapeless. He carefully avoided mentioning the finding of the short stretch of auto track with its V-shaped cut, and the coroner, probably on instructions from the police, refrained from asking him any leading questions.

Fred Strong was then put on the stand for a brief interrogation. The coroner simply wanted him to testify whether or not he had seen a car like the one described by Anderson pass his gas station on the night of the murder. The coroner evidently knew his witness' reputation for taciturnity, so he phrased his questions carefully.

"Now, Mr. Strong," he said judiciously, "in your duties as a vendor of gasoline you doubtless keep a close watch on the road for any cars that might pass. Isn't that so?"

Strong shook his head.

"Why not, Mr. Strong? There aren't many cars on your road. You surely are eager to be on the spot when one does come along."

Fred Strong opened his mouth and actually spoke.

"Let 'em blow if they want gas," he said in a sepulchral voice. "That's what they've got horns for."

There was a titter in the courtroom. The coroner rapped for order.

"Well did you, or did you not, see a car pass your place traveling at high speed just after nightfall on the night that Joseph Hartram was murdered?"

The witness shook his head.

"Answer yes or no," the coroner said sharply.

"Can't," Strong said. "I didn't notice. Somebody went past and then I heard a police motorcycle howlin'."

"But you didn't observe who was in the car?"

Strong muttered a sullen "No" and was excused. He slunk back to his seat and acted as if he had been mortally offended by having been compelled to speak.

As in the Stanton case, the witness who contributed the most actual information was Dr. Sampson, the coroner's physician. He seemed to enjoy testifying. He said that from his examination of the body he had come to the conclusion that the deceased had survived the rather perfunctory strangulation which had been performed, and had actually met his death from the crushing blow of the stone used to smash in the skull. The rope had played no part in the murder. We had evidently frightened the murderer away before he had a chance to use it.

"A blow of this kind would doubtless cause the murderer's person to be stained with blood, wouldn't it?"

The doctor paused judicially. "Yes, in all probability it would. We know from the marks on the stone that his gloves must have become bloodstained. It is very possible that his arms and possibly the upper part of his body would have become spotted."

"In the case of the murder of Howard Stanton, in which you officiated as medical examiner, you said that the deceased had met his death by strangulation, and that the blows on the head, and the hanging of the body took place after death had already occurred, didn't you, Doctor?"

The doctor nodded. "Yes, that is true. In the Stanton case, the strangulation had been performed with great violence and savagery; the blows on the head, although they crushed the skull, were comparatively light."

He drew a long breath and continued:

"In the Hartram case, however, the strangulation would not have caused death. The skull was actually shattered by a single powerful blow with a much heavier stone than the one that had been used on Stanton. I should like to point out that there is a reasonable explanation for this in the very nature of the attack. Stanton, a strong able-bodied man in full possession of all his faculties, was seized from behind by a man who, once he had started, had to subdue his victim. When Stanton became unconscious, we know from a post-mortem examination that he would never have recovered from the effects of the strangulation. The larynx had been fractured. The murderer, of course, could not be certain of this. He smashed the head of his victim several times, probably using the first stone that came to hand—a fairly small one weighing about eight pounds. In the Hartram murder, the intruder throttled a victim, who offered no resistance whatever. The murderer then probably realized how unnecessary such a method of killing was, and crushed in the head with one terrific blow from a rock weighing twenty-three pounds. Whether this rock was brought into the house by the murderer when he first entered, or whether he gave up his effort at strangulation and then obtained the stone, we have no way of knowing. At any rate, the stone was obtained from a wall near the shack and there is some reason to believe that the murderer exercised a deliberate choice. There are many stones in the pile. The one selected by the murderer is heavy, squarish in shape, and ideally suited to his purpose."

"And your conclusion from this is?—"

"A natural one. The Stanton murder, although obviously premeditated, was committed with all the appearance of hatred and anger for the victim. The Hartram murder, which seems to have been committed for the purpose of doing away with a damaging witness to the first murder, was committed with deliberation and cold-blooded efficiency."

"Doesn't it seem that strangulation was a bit unnecessary in the Hartram case?" the coroner asked.

"Frankly it does. However, murderers sometimes have their favorite methods of killing. This one, after realizing that strangulation is a rather difficult and unpleasant way of killing an unconscious man, might well have changed his technique."

"Thank you, Doctor."

The coroner then began his summation of the evidence. He was quite brief, and directed the verdict—which he could hardly help doing—so that the jury quickly came to the unanimous decision that "the deceased came to his death by violence, and that said body has upon it marks of a blow on the head and of strangulation by a person or persons unknown to the jury, and which the jury do find caused the immediate death of said person whose body was found as aforesaid." The foreman went on, unofficially, to link up the murder of Joseph Hartram with that of Howard Stanton, and the court was soon adjourned, much to everybody's relief, for the air in the hot, overcrowded room was becoming unbearable.

We went out into the open. Joan stopped to talk with Miss Harvey. Henry pulled me aside and asked me to help him make a quick inspection of the tires of the cars parked in front of the hotel.

"Don't bother with Fords, Chevrolets, and such small stuff," he said. "The car that was on the Rocky Hill road was a fairly large one. Try that Franklin—Marigold's. It has big husky tires on it."

I tried to look nonchalant as I walked over to Marigold's car to examine its tires as surreptitiously as possible. They were in excellent condition with all the treads intact. Suddenly I heard a voice behind me.

"Those are very good tires, Professor. I've gotten nearly ten thousand miles from them without wearing down the treads."

It was Marigold. I turned to face him and I am afraid that I looked very much like a schoolboy caught stealing apples.

"Are they? They—they look very good," I stammered. "I need some new tires and I haven't quite decided—"

"I can recommend these very highly," he said solemnly. "They have good square treads. No skidding, you know. It's very easy to skid on these dirt roads when they're wet."

I went back to Henry feeling an almost irresistible urge to kick him. He was bending down and squinting at the tires on Dr. Stanton's old LaSalle.

"Come on, let's get out of here," I muttered savagely. "I feel like an awful sap."

"What's the matter, sweetheart? Someone think you were trying to steal his car?" he said, looking up with a cheerful grin.

"You do your own sleuthing: I don't like to go around messing in other people's business. Besides, you're wasting your time. The spare tire on this car hasn't been taken off since the year one."

"You're right," he murmured bending over to examine it carefully. "It's all rusty. Tell me, did you get a chance to look at the Mortons' Buick? They have nice smooth old tires on it."

"No, I didn't," I snapped. "And I'm not going to. Do your own dirty work."

"I did. The tires are just the right size but I couldn't find any V-shaped marks. Of course it's just possible that the part with the mark might be resting on the ground."

"And I suppose you like to have me push the car so the wheels would turn around."

"That's a good idea. Do you suppose?—"

"Go to hell! I'm pushing no cars and I'm—"

"You could creep up behind it with Little Bertha and sort of give it a shove."

I sighed. "Fortunately," I said, "Mr. and Mrs. Morton are now getting into their family vehicle. You might go over and ask them to move the car slowly so you could examine the tires more carefully."

"Mm. That doesn't quite seem to be the right procedure. I guess I'll have to pass up the chance this time. Would you mind if I borrowed Bertha for a while? I want to run up to the Stanton farm with Anderson to trace those feed bags."

CHAPTER XV
HENRY MISSES A RENDEZVOUS

I was all alone in the laboratory when I heard Henry drive up. Joan had gone into the house to help Emma prepare dinner. A moment later he was dashing up the stairs.

"Somebody tried to kill me," he said excitedly as he burst in. "And they've smashed your car."

"What happened? And who is somebody?"

"I don't know. He, it, she, they, or whatever it was got away. But it happened right near here. Between Cal Smith's house and this one."

"Well, calm down and tell me about it."

He sat down on one of the laboratory stools to catch his breath for a moment.

"I was driving back," he said. "I had just passed Cal's house. You know the steep hill on the left side of the road there? Well, I heard something crashing through the bushes. By some lucky reflex action I stepped on the gas and the car shot ahead. Then there was a terrific crash behind me. It shook the whole car. I stopped and got out to look.

"Someone had pushed a big boulder loose and it had been aimed straight for me. The damned thing must be three feet across. It was only my stepping on the gas that saved me. The stone hit the car—smashed in the rumble-seat top, and carried away the rear light and dented the mudguard."

"Maybe it was an accident," I suggested. "Those stones do tear loose sometimes and fall down on the road."

"This was no accident," he said impressively. "I went up the hill to investigate. No one was in sight when I got there, of course, but in the bare spot of ground where the boulder had been, I found this waiting for me."

He held out a crumpled bit of paper. I unfolded it slowly. There was a small round pebble inside and a short bit of string.

I heard Joan calling me. I stuck my head out of the window.

"Little Bertha has been out on a tear," she said, pointing to the wreck.

"I know," I told her. "Somebody tried to drop a rock on Henry, but they squashed Bertha's rear end instead. Come on up and hear about it."

"I'm going to make good for what's happened to your car, of course," Henry said as Joan came up the stairs.

"Don't be foolish," I told him. "It's an old car, anyway. I'll get a second-hand mudguard and rear light and have the rumble-seat top hammered out again. There's nothing to it."

Joan entered the room. "What happened?" she asked Henry.

He told her about the boulder and the note.

"I'm getting scared," she said frankly. "I wonder if you could get your state-trooper friend to spend the night here?"

"That's not a bad idea," said Henry judicially. "He's still over at the Stanton farm. I could go over there and ask him. The car still runs all right, of course. Only the body was damaged."

"Go on," urged Joan. "Invite him to dinner. I'll be awfully glad to have him around."

"I'll go with you," I said. "I want to see the scene of the latest crime."

We went down and I looked sadly at Little Bertha's mangled rear end while Henry turned her around. About a

hundred yards from our house a large boulder was standing at the edge of the road. A trail of crushed underbrush
showed where it had plowed its way down the hillside.
Henry stopped the car and we climbed up to the place
from which the boulder had been pushed.

"There's a good view of the road from here," I said.
"Plenty of time to see a car coming without being seen.
You didn't find any footprints, I suppose?"

"Not a thing," he said. "There's too much undergrowth.
But there's a mark here where our friend must have used a
bar of some kind to start the boulder rolling."

Henry pointed to a mark on the uphill side of the spot
where the boulder had lain.

"See where the hard rock surface underneath is freshly
chipped? That's where he must have thrust a short crowbar. One tug and the stone went crashing downhill with
the pious intention of wiping me out."

Henry pulled out his inevitable camera. He shot close-
ups of the crowbar mark and long shots of the view toward
the road. Then he went downhill to photograph the boulder."

"What did you find out about the Eureka bags?" I
asked, as he snapped the case of his camera shut.

"I'd forgotten all about them," he confessed. "We were
able to locate only four bags in the Stanton barn, so it
seems reasonable to assume that the murderer took the
other one from there."

"It may be a reasonable assumption," I said, "but it's
certainly not a proved fact, and I don't see how it gets you
anywhere."

I was naturally inclined to discount the evidence of the
bags. After all, as Joan had said, it was entirely possible
that the Eureka bag might have been sold as a container
for some farm product during the autumn of the previous
year. Nothing around a farm is more unimportant than an
ordinary burlap sack. Nobody ever notices it; there was
no way of being absolutely certain that it was among the

other bags at the time of Whiskey Joe's murder. Also it was evidently impossible to prove who took it. I explained all this to Henry.

Nevertheless he stuck to his shred of evidence with great stubbornness.

"You never can tell," he said owlishly. "That scrap of burlap may yet be Exhibit A at the trial. Men have been sent to the chair on more trivial evidence than that."

Anderson listened with a grave face to Henry's account of the attack that had been made on him.

"I'll have to phone headquarters," he said. "They like to know where I am. I guess I'd better phone from here. Fammel's is a little too public."

He called Captain Macready from the Stanton house and told him what had happened. He also explained that we had put in a request for police protection for the night. When he hung up he turned to us grinning.

"The captain says that the police protection is okay but he also says that if Sherlock Holmes Junior would go home to New York it wouldn't be needed and we could save the taxpayers some money."

"I'm going away tomorrow," Henry told him. "But I'll be back. I won't be staying with the Whitbys when I return so they won't need any more police protection."

"You're coming back again?" I said incredulously.

"You're crazy!" Anderson told him. "Do you want to get bumped off for sure?"

"I'm not going to let this case drop now," Henry said firmly. "I'm just beginning to get somewhere with it."

"You just turn any dope you have over to us," Anderson said, "and we'll see that it gets taken care of all right."

Henry shook his head. "I'll be back on Tuesday. I've already written the boss asking for a vacation starting then."

Anderson shrugged his shoulders, and kicked his motorcycle engine into action. When we came to the place where the boulder was standing on the road we saw him waving to us from the hillside. We went up to join him and there was a long and fruitless discussion of the boulder-pushing incident.

"I don't think that whoever it was really meant to kill you," I said to Henry finally. "Otherwise he wouldn't have left the warning note here. It seems like an attempt to frighten rather than to kill."

"I told you that that rock just missed me," Henry said vehemently. "If I hadn't—"

"Yes, yes, I know. You told us all about your unconditioned reflexes. Nevertheless it doesn't make sense for a murderer to leave a note of warning after he has killed his man. I still think he just meant to scare you. Perhaps he misjudged his timing and let the rock come too dangerously close."

"We'd better get that boulder off the road anyway," Anderson said. "We can give it another push and let it roll on down into your field."

We performed our duties as citizens and then drove on to the house. Henry suggested that Anderson leave his motorcycle in the garage so it would not stand outside to serve as a public notice that we were under police protection.

Joan welcomed our police escort with great enthusiasm. Emma was very much subdued by the threat that had struck so close to our household and she went about her duties with remarkable silence and reserve. I wished that there were some way of keeping her from spreading the story in the village but I realized that any attempt to keep her quiet would be useless.

Conversation at the dinner table was concerned with a famous kidnaping case in which Anderson had played (according to him) a prominent part. I was grateful for the change of topic because I had heard nothing except talk about our two local murders for days now, and I had come to the point where even a kidnaping case offered some relief. I dragged Joan off to the laboratory as soon as dinner was over since I saw that Henry was determined to spend the evening discussing the details of the murders with Anderson. We worked until nearly midnight, and then, after making Anderson comfortable on the living-room couch, I locked up the house with great care and retired for a night of uneasy rest.

CHAPTER XVI
MR. MARIGOLD'S PSYCHIC CAT

The next day was Sunday and it began with a dismally overcast sky. Before we finished breakfast the rain came down. I was not sorry, though. The dampness would favor the growth of slime molds that could be gathered during the coming week.

Anderson greeted the rain with a glum face. I could hardly blame him. The prospect of having to ride out on a motorcycle in that downpour was not a pleasant one. I invited him to stay with us until the weather improved but he insisted that he had to report to headquarters. He drank a second cup of coffee and went out in the rain. In a few moments he had vanished down the road and our household was left to its usual Sunday-morning routine.

Joan was still asleep as Henry and I leisurely cleaned up the breakfast dishes. The rain pattered down on the roof and blew gustily against the windows. The thought of the trooper on his lonely ride made the dry and cozy kitchen seem even more pleasant than usual.

"You had Anderson to yourself all last evening," I said to Henry who was drying a tumbler with meticulous care. "Did you get him to tell you anything new?"

"He spent most of the time telling me that I ought to go back to New York and stay out of the case. I finally made him agree though that an unofficial investigator planted in the village might be able to pick up some useful information that the police would otherwise never get. I told him I was willing to take a chance so far as getting bumped off is concerned. He offered to get me a permit to carry a gun."

Henry seemed to be quite proud of that.

"You're a lousy shot," I told him. "I don't think you ought to be trusted with a revolver."

"I'm not getting a revolver," he said placidly. "I'm getting a .45 Colt automatic. And I'm not such a bad shot. I just need a little practice."

"Practice? You don't mean to tell me that you expect to go around here firing off a .45 Colt? You could hear it for miles and besides it's dangerous. I'd rather take my chances with the murderer than have you loose in these woods with a heavy gun like that. Those bullets travel quite a distance, you know."

"I don't have to practice around here," he protested. "Anderson invited me to come down to the police range at Fammelton. Said he'd give me some expert instruction, too."

"Why don't you be sensible and stay in New York?"

Henry shook his head stubbornly. "I have a theory about this case now and I want to see if I'm right."

Joan came down a few minutes later. I left her to work on Henry and drove off to get Emma. I gathered from Emma's worried greeting that she had fully expected us to have been murdered in our beds.

"I suppose you told everyone about the boulder that fell downhill yesterday?" I said.

"Fell downhill!" she snorted. "It was pushed and you know it. Somebody was trying to hurt poor Mr. Henry."

"Did you tell everybody about it?"

"Well, Mrs. Morton dropped over to see me last night. And Miss Harvey—"

"That's enough," I sighed. "You did."

"I think they ought to know about it," she said defensively. "There's a murderer in this village and people ought to watch out. Miss Harvey stayed with me last night. She was afraid to be alone and I don't blame her. Do you know Joe Fammel sold out every shotgun shell he had in stock? And a lot of padlocks, too?"

"I'm glad to see that it's helping business," I said. "So the whole village is scared now, eh?"

She smoothed out the fingers of her multicolored gloves and nodded vigorously. "I'm glad Mr. Henry is going to be with me," she said. "It will be a real comfort to have a man in the house."

"Emma," I said seriously, "don't you realize that Mr. Henry's life is in great danger? We have been trying to persuade him to stay in the city. It seems to me that your house, instead of being protected by having him there, would be particularly exposed to attack."

"Good gracious, I hadn't thought of that!" she said uneasily. "Maybe I ought to tell him I can't do it."

"It's for his own good. Mr. Henry is too stubborn to realize it, but it would be much wiser if he were to stay away from this part of the country until this murder case is either solved or forgotten."

"I'll talk to him. I'm going to tell him that it would be too much work to take care of him and look after your house, too."

"That's right," I said virtuously. "You tell him that. It's for his own good. Mrs. Whitby and I are going out to the laboratory in a little while. You get hold of Mr. Henry as soon as we go and explain to him why you can't put him up at your house. You'll really be doing him a favor because he'll be a lot safer if he stays in the city."

Emma naturally was delighted to be a conspirator. A few minutes after we arrived at the house I persuaded Joan to go to the laboratory with me. I told her about what I had said to Emma but she didn't think Henry would be so easily discouraged.

She was right. I had hardly got my first slide in place on the microscope when Henry came bounding up the stairs.

"I can't begin to tell you how much I appreciate your kind efforts in my behalf," he said, "but I'm over twenty-one, sound in mind and body, and quite well able to take care of myself, thank you. Next time, try to get a better accomplice—I got the whole story out of Emma in five minutes. I also persuaded her to let me stay in her house. The gun clinched that. She's thrilled at the idea of having an armed bodyguard around."

"That's very clever of you," I said, squinting into the microscope. "It absolves me of all responsibility. Now when you get killed I won't even have to feel sorry."

"And you can say 'I told you so' at my funeral if that gives you any satisfaction."

"You're both acting very childishly," Joan said. "Henry, why don't you try to be grown up and go back to the city and convert cotton as God doubtless intended you to do?"

There was a loud knock at the downstairs door. I went to the window and leaned out. Someone dressed in yellow oilskins was there. He glanced up as I called out to him. It was Marigold.

"May I come in?" he asked. "I seem to have lost my cat."

"You can come in," I said. "But this isn't that kind of laboratory."

He came up the stairs shaking the rain off his oilskins.

"I wasn't insinuating that Herman had been appropriated for vivisection," he said. "But I thought you might have seen him. He runs off for a spree sometimes, although not usually when it's wet outside."

"That's the deaf cat that goes around smashing glassware, I suppose," Henry said.

"Yes, but he doesn't do it maliciously. He just can't hear things crash. He's really a beautiful cat. A Siamese. Very shy though. He always hides when strangers come to the house. You haven't seen him?"

We all denied ever having seen Herman.

"I should hate to lose him," Marigold went on saying in a worried voice. "Such a lovely cat. Really most unusual. Extraordinarily psychic too—so sensitive to the occult."

"What makes you believe he's psychic?" Henry asked.

"Oh, many, many things. For instance—the morning after Mr. Stanton was murdered I took Herman for a walk up the road. When we passed the place where the body had been found all the hairs stood up on Herman's back and he went around and around me mewing most piteously. Now, how could he have known that a man had just been killed there? I didn't know myself until a few minutes afterwards when I spoke to one of the troopers."

"He might very possibly have smelled the blood that was there," Henry said. "Blood does have an odor, you know—even our insensitive human nostrils are sometimes able to detect it." Henry paused for a moment and then looked at me.

"That's it!" he said. "That would explain it!"

"Explain what?"

"You remember you said you had a vague premonition that something was wrong just before you found Stanton's body? Well, that would explain it, and without any clair-voyant trimmings. You smelled blood! You didn't know what it was—probably you weren't conscious that you smelled anything at all but actually you had detected the odor of blood. And the smell of blood—human blood— ever since the race began, has been associated with disaster and death. No wonder you felt uneasy!"

"It sounds plausible," I admitted.

"But why do you cast aspersions on clairvoyance?" said Marigold.

"Oh, I didn't really. I just meant that I was happier to have a purely mechanistic explanation than to have to take refuge in any of the unproved and still disputed theories of psychic phenomena."

"Have you read about the research work in clairvoy-ance and telepathy that is being done at Duke University?" asked Marigold solemnly.

"Sure. What of it?" said Henry. "What does it prove? Coincidence, if you like."

"Coincidence!" thundered Marigold. "Coincidence on a million-to-one chance computed mathematically?"

"A billion to one if you wish, but better coincidence than the supernatural."

Marigold was almost speechless. He looked to me for support but I said nothing. The argument about the supposedly extra senses of the human mind seems rather futile to me until it can be put on a more scientific plane by careful investigation and controlled research.

"Don't you realize," he said, "that belief in occult manifestations is one of the most widespread of human characteristics? And one of the oldest? Why, every people from—"

"The Solomon Islands to Salem, Massachusetts," Henry helped him out. "Sure I realize it, but don't you think our civilization has advanced to the point where we should be able to cast off such vestiges of savagery?"

"I'm speaking of the scientific validity of extrasensory powers," Marigold said coldly. "I brought in the reference to other races and times only to show how prevalent such manifestations have always been. However, I do think that even such things as witches and werewolves cannot be dismissed contemptuously. The human mind can do strange things. Is it utterly inconceivable that the human will, when directed by malevolence and evil, should be unable to cause madness and death in others?"

"Utterly inconceivable," said Henry firmly.

Marigold looked at him strangely for a moment. "Well, if you think so," he said, "how would you feel if someone, someone versed in those terrible arts, were to undertake a campaign against you? Suppose that someone as skilled in magic as a Congo witch doctor or a Mongolian shaman were to cast one of the ancient spells? Do you think you would escape?"

Henry grinned. "I'd be much more afraid of something substantial—such as a rock."

Marigold looked puzzled for a moment. Then he said:

"Oh yes, I heard about that. Someone pushed a rock downhill and smashed your car. I'm afraid that was done by hands that were all too human. I see nothing of the occult in that. Although there have been cases, of course, where things even larger and heavier than stones were moved by powers that were indisputably not physical."

"I'm glad you think the rock was pushed by human hands," said Henry. "It's hard enough finding the human agencies in this case. I'd hate to have to start chasing spooks as well."

"'Spooks' is such a hideous word," Marigold said with obvious distaste. "There is something vulgar and flauntingly irreverent about it."

"Isn't there though?" Henry agreed cheerfully. "I can see all the astral spirits in the nether world simply quivering with rage every time someone calls them spooks. That's why I like the word. I love to make 'em quiver."

"You shouldn't talk that way," Marigold protested seriously. "You may be inviting trouble. You know even some of our greatest scientists are beginning to believe now. Have you read Alexis Carrel's new book? You can't pooh-pooh a man like Carrel."

"I've read it," Henry said grinning. "And I still don't believe in fairies—not the kind he talks about anyway."

Our guest had stomped angrily down the stairs in search of his cat.

Joan suppressed a giggle. "I don't think you were very nice to him," she said to Henry.

"These old-maidish dabblers in the occult give me a pain. Psychic cats, my eye!"

"Well," I told him, "you can expect to wilt away and die now as soon as our spell-casting friend gets his wax image of you under way."

"I'm more afraid of getting bopped on the head with a rock. I'm glad I thought about that business of the blood odor, though. It's an interesting point."

"It may be interesting but I don't see how it is going to help you establish who the murderer is. You've got a lot of work to clean up on this case yet. What train do you expect to get tonight?"

"There's one leaving Whitechurch at 8:37 daylight time. It would get me in town at a reasonably early hour. Meanwhile may I borrow your typewriter? I want to type up some notes on the case before I leave."

CHAPTER XVII
"I'VE GOT HIM ON THE LIST"

Joan and I finished our work in the laboratory late in the afternoon. We found Henry seated at a bridge table in the living room with my typewriter in front of him. There were several badly typed pages spread out on the table. Henry was evidently trying to transcribe information from his little notebook.

"If I could only read my own handwriting," he complained as we entered the room, "I'd have a complete dossier on this case. This notebook contains a wealth of pertinent information taken down on the spot but I can't make out most of it!"

Joan made the proper sympathetic noises. "Let's see what you've written anyway," she said making a dive for the typewritten sheets.

Henry made no effort to stop her but he seemed to be rather uncomfortable.

"I don't think you ought to read that," he protested feebly. "It's really confidential and besides you may not like what it says."

"Nonsense," she said, seating herself in an armchair and starting to read. "Why shouldn't I see it? I know all about the case."

I leaned over her shoulder and we rapidly skimmed over several pages that summarized the story of the two murders. Then Joan turned a new page and we saw this elaborate list of suspects and their possible alibis:

THE HOUSE OF STANTON

	Access to car?	Access to phone?	Alibi in Stanton case?	Alibi in Hart-ram case?	Physically able to commit murder?
MRS. ADA DENNER, *housekeeper;* widow, age about 34. Emma hints that she was Stanton's mistress. Possible jealousy motive?	Yes but doesn't drive	Yes	Yes	Yes	Probably
GEORGE HATHAWAY, *farmhand;* age about 40 or more. Physically strong but not very bright. Possible sex tie-up with Mrs. Denner? Might have done away with Stanton and called my host in to discover the body, but he hardly seems to have	Yes	Yes	Yes, but not a water-tight one	Yes	Yes

	Access to car?	Access to phone?	Alibi in Stanton case?	Alibi in Hartram case?	Physically able to commit murder?
the imagination for such a stunt.					
DR. ALLEN STANTON, age about 50. Couldn't have killed his brother as he was definitely in Cleveland at the time. Inheritance motive possible but it hardly seems likely that he would have killed Whiskey Joe to shield his brother's murderer.	Yes	Yes, but not on village party line	Yes	No	Yes
FRED STRONG, age about 45. Related by marriage to the Stantons. Keeps a gas station on the Calverton road.	Yes	Yes, but not on village party line	No	No	Yes
JENNIE STRONG, his wife; age somewhere over 40. Most unattractive and completely dominated by her husband.	Yes	Yes	No	No	Yes

THE HOUSE OF WHITBY

JAMES WHITBY, age 35. Might very well have killed	Yes	No	No	Yes	Yes

	Access to car?	*Access to phone?*	*Alibi in Stanton case?*	*Alibi in Hart-ram case?*	*Physically able to commit murder?*
Stanton out of sheer maliciousness or scientific curiosity but I know he didn't kill Whiskey Joe.					
JOAN WHITBY, his wife, age under 30. Attractive. No alibis. Might have done away with both of them—but then why should she?	No	No	No	No	Perhaps
EMMA BIRCH, age 55(?). No alibis but couldn't do the strangling—or could she?	No	No	No	No	Perhaps

CITIZENS AT LARGE

JOSEPH FAMMEL, *storekeeper,* age about 35. Had falling-out with Stanton. Was in his own house a few minutes after we discovered Whiskey Joe's body. Since Anderson was at that moment pursuing a north-bound automobile,	Yes	Yes	No	Yes	Yes

	Access to car?	Access to phone?	Alibi in Stanton case?	Alibi in Hartram case?	Physically able to commit murder?
Fammel has a per- fectly good alibi.					
MRS. FAMMEL, his wife, over 30. Ditto.	Yes	Yes	No	Yes	Yes
HENRY MORTON, age about 55. Don't know much about the gentleman. His wife was at the Stanton house on the day of the in- quest. She might have swiped the Eureka bag for him. Must investi- gate this family.	Yes	Yes	No	No	Yes
MRS. HENRY MOR- TON, age well over 50. Church leader, W. C. T. U. presi- dent, and general busybody. All the qualifications need- ed for murder. Must establish a good motive for her, though. She evidently listened in on the phone and heard that Stanton was in the field on night of murder.	Yes	Yes	No	No	Probably

	Access to car?	*Access to phone?*	*Alibi in Stanton case?*	*Alibi in Hart- ram case?*	*Physically able to commit murder?*
Miss Alice Harvey, *spinster*, age about 70. No alibis, but if she can lift a twenty-three-pound stone, I'll let her hit me with it.	No	Yes	No	No	No
Ramsey Morgan, age about 56. Was in the army with Stanton. Out of town on the night of Stanton murder though.	Yes	Yes	Yes	No	Yes
Anna Morgan, age well over 45. Rather stout. Housewife. I know nothing about her, really.	Yes	Yes	No	No	Probably not
Bill Morgan, son of above. Age under 25. Don't know much about him. Must find out more.	Yes	Yes	No	No	Yes
Mary Morgan, his wife, age about 22. Ditto.	Yes	Yes	No	No	Perhaps
David Hamlin, age about 58. Lives conveniently near	Yes	Yes	Yes	No	Yes

	Access to car?	Access to phone?	Alibi in Stanton case?	Alibi in Hart-ram case?	Physically able to commit murder?
Stanton and Whiskey Joe but nothing else against him. At party on night of Stanton's murder.					
MINNA HAMLIN, his sister, age over 50. Vague rumors from Emma that Stanton had once cast sheep's eyes at her. At party with her brother on night of Stanton murder.	Yes	Yes	Yes	No	Yes
EDGAR A. HARMON, age about 55. Was in army with Stanton. Suspected that he might be shamming invalidism, but he was nearly burned alive last winter when a cigarette set his bed on fire and he couldn't get out.	No	No	No	Yes	No
EMMETT HARMON, his son. Irresponsible, but couldn't do strangling because of paralyzed hand.	No	No	No	Yes	No
JOHN C. MILLER, age about 65. Bach-	No	Yes	Yes	No	Yes

	Access to car?	Access to phone?	Alibi in Stanton case?	Alibi in Hartram case?	Physically able to commit murder?
elor. Lives alone. Had a fight with Stanton over land boundaries and was not on speaking terms with him although he was his nearest neighbor. At party with Hamlins on night of Stanton murder.					
CALEB SMITH, age about 60. Widower. Lives alone. Was best friend of Whiskey Joe's. Out of town with Ramsey Morgan on night of Stanton murder.	No	No	Yes	No	Yes
ERNEST L. MARIGOLD, bachelor, age about 45. Retired city person living on an income. Previous vocation unknown; source of income unknown. Interested in curious subjects such as torture and the occult.	Yes	No	No	No	Yes

"You've got an awful nerve," said Joan. "Putting us down on that list."

"Why not?" Henry countered blithely. "Everybody around here is a suspect. Why, the coroner even tried to hang Whiskey Joe's murder on me! I ought to be on the list myself."

"Will you let me write your description?" Joan asked sweetly.

"Sure, go ahead."

Joan took a pencil and wrote:

> Henry Hale, age 34. The last person to see Whiskey Joe alive. Actions suspicious through-out case. Known to have a morbid interest in murder. Probably did it out of depraved curiosity.

"You can add your own tabular matter," she said.

"You know, Henry," I said, "your list is very pretty and apparently inclusive, but after all there is an excellent possibility that the murders were committed by someone not in this immediate vicinity—someone whose name you don't even know—whose existence you don't even suspect."

"Don't I know it!" he said, sighing. "But I can't be a combination state police force, Pinkerton Agency, and Scotland Yard all in one. I have to work within human limitations."

"Well, I wish you luck, but don't forget the great unknowns outside."

"You'll never solve it," Joan said scornfully. "The police will have the murderer in jail before you untangle your own handwriting." And with that she left us and went into the kitchen.

Henry spread out the six sheets of his typewritten list on the table and began to pore over them.

"You know," he said, "when I get all these people drawn up on a list like this, it becomes evident that I must come back here to do more work on the case. Why, there are half a dozen of them that I know hardly anything about. Take the Strongs, for instance. What do I know about them? I've seen them and I've passed their gas station but I've never had a chance to talk with them. The police have questioned them, of course. They claim to have alibis on both nights but I can see possible loopholes. They sold gas to several people who knew them and who can attest to their presence at the gas station. Unfortunately he sold the gas to some, and she sold it to others. With a little close co-operation he could easily have gotten away long enough to commit the murders. She could cover him by pretending that he was in the house while she held a one-sided conversation with him. It's an old trick, of course, although Mrs. Strong isn't exactly the type I'd pick to be an actress."

"It wouldn't be much of a trick to hold a one-sided conversation with Fred Strong," I said. "It's the only way you can talk to him."

"I must find out more about them," he said. "After all, they're relatives of the Stantons; They're next in line for the estate after the doctor. And then, some of these other birds—the police have checked their alibis and Anderson tipped me off about some of them. They found out that there had been a party in Whitechurch the evening of the Stanton murder. Dave Hamlin and his sister and J. C. Miller were present. I suppose that lets them out. None of them were very likely suspects anyway."

"I noticed that you had some kind of party alibis checked for them on your list," I said.

"As for the others," Henry went on, "Cal Smith and Ramsey Morgan were down in the southern part of the state when Stanton was killed. They were looking at a bird dog. They didn't get home until after eleven. The man who owned the dog attested to the fact that they hadn't left his place until after nine. Which was pretty decent of him considering the fact that they didn't buy the dog."

"Well," I said, consulting the list, "that leaves such people as Mr. and Mrs. Morton, young Bill Morgan and his wife, and Mr. Marigold wide open for suspicion."

"Mr. Marigold is perfect for a murderer, of course. And he has no alibis at all. He told the police he was home reading when both Stanton and Whiskey Joe were killed. But I don't think he killed them. He talks a good murder but I can't see his soft, flabby hands throttling anyone. Mr. Morton was in the army with Stanton. That may have some significance. It needs looking into anyway. As for his wife," he added viciously, "nothing would please me better than to get something on that old cow!"

"No such luck," I said. "I'm afraid Mrs. Morton isn't the type that would commit open-handed murder. She might nag someone to death but I can't imagine her killing with her own two hands. Besides, what motive would she have?"

"What motive has anybody?"

"I thought you said you had a theory that might explain the whole thing."

"I thought I did too. But it's pretty strange. It will take a lot of thinking about and meanwhile I need more clues— more evidence."

"Well, how about alibis for the night of Whiskey Joe's murder?"

"Hardly anyone seems to have a good alibi for that night," Henry said despairingly. "Everybody was at home. The whole village was afraid to go out because there was a murderer at large. There are plenty of interfamily alibis, of course, but even the police agree that they don't mean much."

The rain continued to come down. Emma and Joan put themselves out to make a very special Sunday dinner for which we had reserved the Chateau Margaux, but none of us could work up an appetite, so the meal fell rather flat.

A few minutes before eight I packed Emma and Henry into the car. I dropped Emma off at her house and drove Henry through the pouring rain to the station where he caught his train to New York.

CHAPTER XVIII
BLONDE AND BEAUTIFUL

Monday and Tuesday were blissfully free from outside interruptions. The police investigation was still going on but I wasn't disturbed. I ignored the neighborhood gossip and even Emma's attempts at conversation. I worked sixteen hours a day to clear away everything on my desk, so as to be free for the business of collecting new specimens. The weather was still rainy on Monday and Tuesday was dampish. The long dry spell had ended and growth conditions were ideal for a good crop of slime molds.

I drove down to Whitechurch in high spirits on Tuesday evening to meet Helen and Henry at the train. The western sky was clearing; brilliant sunset colors touched the clouds and gave promise of fair weather. I was looking forward to a ramble through the fields and woods with Joan and Helen in search of new material.

Helen is an extraordinarily pleasant person to have around. She is not very tall—not much over five feet—but she has a perfectly proportioned figure, a clear white skin, and spectacularly beautiful golden hair. Pullman porters, taxi drivers, bootblacks, and small boys pay her homage wherever she goes. She always makes a stir whenever she enters a restaurant or a theater, and in college she was as popular with the faculty as she was with the students—male students, that is. She deserved the high marks she got, though, for she really worked for them. She possesses a remarkable talent for biology—she has a sympathy and

understanding for everything that grows, from wild flowers to the humble microscopic slime molds that I specialize
in. Needless to say, I was delighted to have her spend part
of her summer vacation with us as my laboratory assistant.

The gates were lowered soon after I drove into the station yard and I heard the train whistle far away down the
track. It drew up with much blowing of steam and loud
noises. I saw Helen, dressed in gay sports clothes, waving
to me from the platform of the last car. She ran across the
cinders toward me while Henry plodded behind laden with
bags.

"Well, you seem to have become acquainted, all right,"
I told her.

"It was awfully nice of you to have Henry meet me and
help me out," Helen said.

I raised an incautious eyebrow.

"We decided not to be formal since we were going to be
out here together," she explained.

"Did he talk to you about Myxomycetes?"

"He tried to," she laughed, "but I switched the conversation to murder. He really does know a lot about murders. He told me how someone had tried to kill him by
throwing a rock down on your car. Golly, it certainly did
get smashed, didn't it?"

Henry came up with the bags and I could see from the
silly expression on his face that Helen had made a fatal
impression on him. He greeted me solemnly and said not
one word about the murder!

Helen got in and pushed over close to me so Henry
could sit up front with us. We started off up the long hill
that leads to Brookdale.

"I suppose Henry has given you a detailed and dia-
grammed description of our local murders," I said to Helen.

"Yes, he has," she said seriously. "I think he has been
doing some very fine work and it's certainly brave of him
to come back here after his life has been threatened."

I managed to catch a glimpse of Henry's reddening face as I shifted down to second gear on the hill.

"The police have been at a standstill while he has been away," I said gravely. I could see Henry wince.

"Have you seen Anderson at all?" he asked abruptly.

"No, I haven't," I said. "I've been glad to have this respite from murder so I could get some work done. I haven't seen anybody. We'll be able to do some specimen gathering tomorrow," I said, turning to Helen. "This rain will have made conditions just right."

"Hasn't Emma had anything to say?" he persisted.

"She got hold of me as I was leaving the house and asked me to tell you that Mrs. Morton has been dropping hints about knowing something."

"Mrs. Morton had better watch out or she'll find herself the center of attraction at another inquest," Henry said. "It's not very healthy to know too much about those murders. Just what did she say?"

"Nothing very definite. Something about how we might all be surprised if we knew what she knew and that you could never tell about people even though you practically lived next door to them all your life."

"What do you suppose she meant by that?"

"I don't know. That's all Emma said."

"I wish somebody would speak out loud and bold just for once about this affair. There seems to be a whispering campaign going on so far as evidence is concerned. First there was Whiskey Joe with his veiled suggestions. Well, he was drunk, so there's some excuse for him. But don't tell me that Mrs. Morton has been drinking!"

"Mrs. Morton," I explained to Helen, "is the president of our local W.C.T.U. I did once hear a story, however, that she got so drunk on punch at her own wedding she passed out and didn't wake up till the next day."

"Mrs. Morton would get drunk at a time like that," Henry chuckled. "I wonder whether she really knows anything about this affair or whether she's just trying to act important."

"Why don't you ask her?" Helen asked, sensibly enough, I thought.

"I fully intend to, Mademoiselle. I fully intend to."

We were almost in Brookdale.

"There's no use dropping you off at Emma's house now," I said to Henry. "There's nobody home. You come up to our place and have dinner with us."

He offered no objection and in another few minutes we drove up in front of our house. Joan and Tinkel were waiting for us.

Helen had never been out for an extended visit before. Joan took her up to her room while Henry insisted on interviewing Emma about Mrs. Morton's mysterious statements. He was able to find out nothing more definite than what I had already told him.

When Emma had finished washing the dinner dishes Henry drove her home and took his luggage along. We had invited him to spend the evening with us after he had unpacked and settled himself in his new quarters. During his absence Joan told Helen about his good qualities, many of which were new to me. I had never suspected that a woman would consider him good-looking—in fact, I had never thought about the matter at all. He does, I suppose, have a certain careless charm of manner and a superficial knowledge of many trivial subjects that might impress the average woman, but I had thought that both Joan and Helen, who were trained in scientific observation, would be able to judge him better. Women, it seems, have curious blind spots when it comes to judging men rather than laboratory specimens.

Henry did not return until it was almost dark, and when he entered our living room he was red-faced and angry.

"The old bitch!" he burst out. "She practically shut the door in my face!"

"Who?" asked Joan patiently. "Emma?"

"No, of course not! That scandal-mongering old hypocrite, Mrs. Morton. She told me that she would give any information she might have to the properly constituted authorities at the proper time and place. She'd damned well better, too, or I'll get the police after her for suppressing evidence." Joan and Helen were very sympathetic but I couldn't help feeling that there was some justification for Mrs. Morton's stand. After all, Henry was an outside interloper concerning himself unasked in a very serious local affair.

The next morning, Joan, Helen, and I set out for a specimen-gathering expedition. Henry had suggested that we spend some time in the fields and woods around the scenes of the murders in the hope that we might come across something. Since this locale was as satisfactory as any for the growth of Myxomycetes, I was willing enough to humor him.

He had determined to spend the day at Fammelton where he hoped to see Anderson and also look up some data in the local library. I lent him our car for the purpose. He promised to have a mechanic work on its shattered body while he was in town.

We took our lunch with us and spent the day in the open. The pursuit of scientific knowledge can be very pleasant indeed when there are two charming young ladies for company and an idyllic landscape for a setting. We collected many interesting-looking specimens, but, as I had expected, we discovered no new murder clues of any kind.

Henry returned from Fammelton about four and came in search of us. We sat down on a sunny hillside overlooking Brookdale to listen to his latest revelations.

"Did you see Anderson?" I asked.

Henry shook his head sadly. "He was in court testifying about something or other so I missed him. I went to the Fammelton Library though and spent hours looking up local history.

"I waded through the files of the Hampton County *Rocket* from 1895 to date. It's a four-page weekly, so it wasn't such a terrible job. I turned up a few odds and ends which may or may not have some bearing on the case."

He pulled out several slips of paper from his pocket.

"For instance, there were seven men from this vicinity who were in the Spanish-American War. Two of them died some time ago. I came across their obits, so they don't count. The five who do are Howard Stanton, Ramsey Morgan, Edgar Harmon, Henry Morton, and Cal Smith.

"I also found out the date of Stanton's marriage was June 6, 1906. His wife died in 1917 under circumstances that sound like possible suicide but no fuss was raised about it at the time. Edgar Harmon's wife did kill herself though. Right after the birth of their idiot son. She tried to kill the child by suffocating him with a pillow, but they managed to bring him to, which seems rather unnecessary to me. However, that's a matter of civilization and ethics that we won't go into now.

"In 1923 Stanton bought his tenant farm at a sheriff's sale for six hundred dollars which is quite a bargain. It had been owned by one Ralph Denner who died in 1922. Stanton took his widow in as housekeeper after this purchase of the tenant farm. There's a thought there all right.

"I came across something that has no direct bearing on the case but it opens up an interesting line of speculation. In the spring of 1918, the body of a young man who had died of exposure during the winter was found in a shack on the mountain. He had evidently lived there for some time and the presence of a quantity of tin cans and newspapers showed that someone had evidently been bringing supplies to him from the outside. The *Rocket* suggested that he might have been a draft evader. He was never identified. The whole business doesn't mean anything, of course, but it does show that someone could live on that mountain, unobserved and unknown, for a long time. Such a person, a maniac perhaps, might have descended on the village and—"

"One of my great unknowns," I commented.

"It might be," Henry said soberly. "But I hope not."

"Anything else?"

"I found out that three legal suits had been entered at various times against Howard Stanton. One was started by a dairy company. It didn't sound very interesting. The other two are more promising. One, which is still pending, was brought against him by Ramsey Morgan on a matter of alleged fraud in the sale of a bull. Morgan claimed that the bull was sterile. The other suit was started by our silent friend, Fred Strong. The case was settled out of court."

"What kind was it?"

"Oh, some long-drawn-out and dismal business about the sale of land. I gathered that Strong bought his gas station site from Howard. But that isn't what was interesting about it. What struck me was that the two men actually came to blows about it. They had a fist fight in the main street of Fammelton just before they went into a lawyer's office to settle the case. Curiously enough, they actually did settle it."

"Well, you can find out from some of the people around here just what it was all about if you think it really is important. They won't have forgotten the affair, I can promise you. Nothing more to tell us about?"

"No, I guess not. I got a lot of interesting dope about an Indian encampment that was on the mountain some two hundred years ago, and I read all about the capture of a Hessian soldier in one of the houses still standing on the Marbury road, but neither of these facts seems to be very pertinent."

"There's an awful lot of waste motion investigating a murder, isn't there?" Helen asked naively.

"About 99 per cent," Henry confessed. "But that's the way things are. I've had your car fixed up," he said to me, "but she still looks pretty seedy. I'm afraid she'll carry the scars to her grave."

We went back to the house for a dip in the brook. Helen looked very handsome in a bright blue bathing suit, but I was not permitted to enjoy her company for very long. Joan had to leave early in order to help Emma prepare dinner and she signaled to me, in the secret but peremptory way that wives have, to accompany her to the house so the two would be left together. I must admit that they didn't seem to notice my absence.

As I was dressing, I accused Joan of open-handed and deliberate matchmaking.

"Henry is thirty-four years old," she said. "He's a nice boy and there's no reason why he shouldn't get married."

"I'm not worried about Henry. He can take care of himself. But I don't want to see my laboratory assistant snatched away from me in the middle of the summer. I've trained Helen for this work and I don't intend to be deprived of her services by a cotton-converting would-be sleuth!"

"I suppose it would be rather difficult for you to get another laboratory assistant right now, wouldn't it?" she said with deceptive consideration.

"It certainly would," I agreed cheerfully.

"Especially one so charming and attractive as Helen!"

"I don't see what that's got to do with it."

"Of course not. I've always been certain that it was only coincidence that you picked Helen out of your class to specialize in mycology. She's bright, interested in the subject, and a conscientious worker. You never noticed, of course, that she's also a damned good-looking girl!"

"You're making a perfect fool of yourself," I said calmly. "I hope you're not going to be jealous all of a sudden. And I think your efforts to foist Helen on Henry are childish and much too obvious. You're making them both very uncomfortable."

I turned to make a dignified exit and received Joan's wet bathing suit on the back of my neck, right on the clean collar I had just put on.

We were both very late for dinner, but Henry and Helen were even later.

During the evening I retired to a corner and read some of the Saki stories. They were a decided relief from the incessant atmosphere of murder that was engrossing my household, Henry, Joan, and Helen sat around a bridge table and studied the list of suspects. Then Helen, who has a very workmanlike and orderly mind, got the idea of transcribing the list on filing cards for Henry's convenience. They stayed there until late in the night shifting the cards around in little piles representing very suspicious, possible, and unlikely persons. It all seemed very foolish to me.

I was really convinced that Henry, as a lone and inexperienced investigator, had a very slight chance of solving two murders that had completely stumped a large and reasonably efficient police force. I was as familiar with the evidence as he was and I was certainly much better acquainted with all the local people who might have committed the crime. None of them seemed to fit. The only person in the whole community who was vicious enough to have had the necessary potentialities for murder was Howard Stanton himself.

CHAPTER XIX
I STEP ON SOMETHING

The weather held clear for the next day, so we repeated our specimen-collecting expedition. This time we went beyond the Rocky Hill road and searched the woods which begin there. Henry drove us to the fork in the road and then went off on some mysterious errand of his own.

The woods in which we were working start at the edge of a cleared field beyond the road. The field is part of the Hamlin farm so I felt perfectly free to trespass there since Dave Hamlin has always been very friendly to me. The woods, though, belong to the Stanton estate. I had explored them before, but Howard Stanton had never seen me there, so I had never been molested. I did not know how his heir presumptive, Dr. Allen Stanton, would feel about our trespassing on the property which he had inherited, but it seemed likely that he might be more sympathetic to scientific research than his brother.

Joan and Helen were looking for material in a pile of decayed leaves in the shelter of a large boulder. I left them there and followed a low wall of loose stones that ran along the edge of the forest. Embedded in the stones was the rotted stump of a large tree. I poked it with a stick; a piece of the stump split off, exposing the soft brown decayed wood. It seemed to be an excellent place for slime molds to grow, so I climbed up eagerly on the stone row to examine it more closely.

In my haste to get to it I neglected to watch my footing closely and to my indescribable terror I felt something squirm under my foot. There was a flash of brown and I saw an ugly mottled snake, unmistakably a copperhead, sink its fangs viciously into the leather boot I was wearing. I struck at it with the stick as I leaped away and succeeded in crippling it so that it threshed about angrily. I picked up one of the stones and sent it crashing down on its head. The broken body continued to wriggle spasmodically.

I stripped off my belt to make a tourniquet and called to Joan in as level a voice as was possible under the circumstances. There must have been something in the way I spoke that frightened her though, because she came running up, white-faced and panicky.

"I've been struck by a copperhead," I said as calmly as I could. "Will you get me a short stick while I strap this belt around my leg?"

She stood there clutching at her blouse and looking at me with large, terror-stricken eyes. Then without a word she picked up the long stick that I had hit the snake with and broke it over her knee. She thrust the short piece through the strap and twisted it to shut off the circulation. She almost wrenched my leg off.

"For Christ's sake, go easy!" I yelled. "You're worse than the snake. Unlace the boot and let's see how bad it is."

I knew the snake had struck through the boot since my foot had immediately begun to pain me. Joan tore at the laces with frantic haste. Helen came running up.

"I've been bitten by a copperhead," I said to Helen. "Run down to the main road. The first house on the other side is the Stanton place. You can see it from here—a big white house with red barns. There's just a chance the doctor may be in. If he's not, they have a telephone, so you can call him."

Helen dashed off as Joan succeeded in drawing off the boot. She ripped off the sock. There were two tiny pin-holes, just above the toes.

I clutched the stick of the tourniquet, easing up on it occasionally so as not to shut off the circulation entirely.

"There's a knife in my right-hand pocket," I said. "Get it and open up the flesh around the bite and then squeeze the blood out."

Joan looked at me miserably and then obeyed.

I gritted my teeth as she sliced into the living flesh. The blood oozed out thick and discolored. She soaked it up with a handkerchief.

"Squeeze it out," I said faintly, with a horrible sick feeling in the pit of my stomach. The air surged up black around me. Then I heard the doctor's hearty voice and looked up to find him bending over me with an old-fashioned tubular stethoscope.

"It's all right," Joan was whispering, "the doctor says it isn't bad at all. He's going to give you an injection of antivenin."

She unbuttoned my shirt and the doctor quickly sunk the needle into the soft flesh of the abdomen. Helen handed me something to drink in a little metal cup.

The doctor replaced my makeshift tourniquet with a bandage. He drew out some kind of instrument from his case and went to work on the wound.

"I guess we can manage to get him down to the road," the doctor said. "Now, young lady, if you'll take my bag—"

Joan and the doctor made a seat with their arms and picked me up with some difficulty. Helen followed with the doctor's bag and my boot. Joan staggered under the load but they finally got me down to the road. George Hathaway came running up and relieved Joan of my weight.

A few minutes later I was in the parlor of the Stanton house lying on a horsehair sofa. Mrs. Denner and the doctor bustled around. Joan suddenly began to cry. Helen led her out of the room.

"It's all right, take it easy now," the doctor said cheerfully. "This is really a very slight affair. Your leather boot saved you from getting much of the poison. I'm surprised the snake was able to bite through at all."

He picked up the boot. "See, here's where he got you," he said, pointing to the toe. "There's a crack here—it's a pretty old boot—or he wouldn't have gotten through."

Helen came in and whispered to the doctor who immediately left the room with her.

"Where's my wife?" I demanded irritably. "Is there something wrong with her now?"

Mrs. Denner went out and came back a few minutes later with Joan and the doctor. Joan's eyes were red and as she bent over me I could smell whiskey.

"Hey, what's the idea?" I demanded. "I've got the snake bite. Why don't I get the whiskey?"

"That's an exploded theory," said the doctor smiling. "There's no point in giving a stimulant. We want to keep the blood quiet—not stir it up."

Joan swayed unsteadily and then sat down hard.

"He gave me an awfully big shot of it," she said. Then she quietly hiccoughed.

Dr. Stanton insisted that I must spend the night in his house so he could keep an eye on the progress of my recovery. Henry put in an appearance late in the afternoon. He greeted me in somewhat awestruck tones and tiptoed around the parlor as though I were on the point of death. Joan was sleeping off the whiskey the doctor had given her, but she roused herself drowsily when Henry came in.

"The doctor has some awfully good Scotch," she told him. "Why don't you go and help yourself to a drink? It'll brace you up. There's a whole decanter of it on the sideboard in the next room."

"I can't just go and help myself," Henry said awkwardly.

"Sure you can," she urged. "Go and get it. The doctor's a good scout. He won't mind. I'll have one, too."

"You will not," I said determinedly.

Joan's mouth tightened into a stubborn line.

"I really don't think you ought to have any more, Mrs. Whitby," the doctor said, suddenly appearing in the door-way with a decanter and a glass. "Doctor's orders. But let me offer you some," he said, turning to Henry.

Joan slumped into her chair.

"Doctor Stanton, this is Mr. Hale," I said, introducing them.

Henry shook hands with the doctor and then took the proffered glass and downed the liquor at a gulp.

"How's the patient, Doctor? They tell me he's going to recover."

"He'll come around all right. He's over the worst of it already. A little quiet, a few days in bed, and he'll be back on his feet again as chipper as ever."

He was looking at Henry curiously.

"You're the young man who has interested himself in try-ing to solve the mystery of my brother's death, aren't you?"

"Oh, in an amateur sort of way," Henry said with some embarrassment.

"Perhaps I can be of some assistance to you," the doctor said. "I'd like to see this thing cleared up. I've already given the police access to my brother's papers and personal things. They saw nothing of any significance but if you'd like to have a look at them, I'd be glad to show them to you."

"That's swell of you," Henry said.

"Suppose we go through the stuff after dinner then," the doctor suggested.

Dinner was served early according to country custom. After it was over, the doctor insisted on my going to sleep, so I missed the examination of Howard Stanton's personal effects. Henry and Joan came into the parlor about eleven. I had been sleeping lightly and I opened my eyes as they entered.

"What did you find?" I asked rather eagerly.

"Forget about it," Henry said. "You get a good night's rest and I'll tell you all about it tomorrow. There isn't a lot to tell though, so don't think about it too much."

"I'm going to sleep here on a cot," Joan whispered in the hushed tone that people always use in the sickroom.

"And what about Henry and Helen?"

"They're going back to the house to sleep."

I sat up quickly. "They can't do that," I protested. "You'll have the whole town talking. And besides—"

Joan pushed me back gently.

"Don't worry about it, Mr. Grundy. Emma will be there to chaperone them."

Henry grinned wickedly at me as Joan pushed him out of the room.

I awoke early in the morning. It was a cloudy and dismal day that threatened rain at any moment. Joan was up as soon as she heard me stirring. She came over to my bed to inquire solicitously how I felt.

"I'm all right," I said grumpily. "I feel fine and there's no reason why I shouldn't get up."

"You'll wait until the doctor sees you, that's what you'll do," she said. "He said you have to stay in bed for a few days."

"I've got work to do," I complained. "I can't waste my life lying in bed."

"You can keep right on working in bed as soon as you get home. I'll bring you your manuscript and you can write all day long—if the doctor will let you. We're going to move you back to the house this morning if everything is all right."

Shortly before noon Henry brought the car around for me. The doctor came in to give me a final examination before letting me go home. He felt my pulse, listened to my heart with his stethoscope, and then uncovered and examined the wound.

"I guess you'll be all right," he said at last. "Stay in bed for a few days, though. I'll drop over to see you tomorrow."

I thanked him for his hospitality as well as for his medical care and asked him to send me his bill. Then Henry, who had been watching everything with great interest, helped me hobble out to the car. In a few minutes I was home. Helen greeted me with great solicitude and she assisted Joan in making me comfortable.

Henry came up to the bedroom to talk to me as soon as lunch was over. We plunged immediately into a discussion of what he had found out from the doctor.

"The most important thing," he began, "is the fact that Howard died without leaving a will. Anderson told me as much yesterday and the doctor confirmed it. It seems that his brother was terribly afraid of dying and had a superstitious dislike of anything concerned with death. His attorney, a local man in Calverton, had urged Stanton several times to make a will but he always put it off. So the whole estate, of course, goes to the doctor.

"The doctor told me also that Mrs. Denner had been living—shall we say in sin—with his brother. She has no legal claim of any kind on the estate, of course, but he has arranged to give her an income, which I think is rather decent of him."

I nodded. "What else?"

"Well, I cleared up the matter of the check which was found in Whiskey Joe's pocket. I saw the stub in Stanton's checkbook. It was marked 'Liquor.'"

"Mm. I said as much at the time."

"I know you did. That's about all I found that might have any direct bearing on the case, but I had a long talk with the doctor about his brother. He was quite frank. He admitted that Howard had an ungovernable temper and an absolute disregard for the feelings of other people. If he had gotten into a row with someone the night he was murdered, he might very well have goaded such a person bn to the point of attacking him. But we know that by the very nature of the attack he must have been taken by surprise. I wonder why the murderer picked on that particular night to kill Stanton? It's true that it was known he was going to be alone in the hayfield until dark. But there was nothing unusual in that. It's possible enough, of course, that Stanton may have had a recent set-to with someone we don't know about. Or, it might have been the great unknown from the outside that you're always hinting at. I'm beginning to lose a little faith in my own theory, you see."

"You worry about it," I said. "I've got enough troubles of my own right now. Will you ask Joan to bring up my manuscript?"

CHAPTER XX
THE NEXT MAN TO DIE?

Dr. Stanton arrived about eleven o'clock the next morning to make his promised call. He came into the bedroom with the air of professional cheerfulness that doctors evidently feel it necessary to display.

"A glorious day, Mr. Whitby. A little warm outside but . . . pulse almost normal. Let's see your foot."

I stuck my foot out. He unwrapped the bandages and gazed at the ugly-looking wound.

"Very nice," he said judiciously. "Very nice, indeed. Hardly any swelling and no signs of infection. You ought to throw this off very quickly."

He finished bandaging my foot.

"What's this?" he said, suddenly pointing to my manuscript.

"A book I'm writing on the Myxomycetes of this state. Are you interested in Myxomycetes?"

"No, can't say that I am especially. I haven't even heard the term since I studied biology in college. Some sort of little gadgets, aren't they?"

"Microscopic slime molds. Perhaps you'd like to look at the manuscript? It may revive fond memories of your college years."

"I have no fond memories of my college years," he said, idly turning the pages. "My father died before I got out of college. My brother promptly cut off my allowance and I had to work my way through."

He studied the manuscript intently for a few minutes.

"My brother," he said, turning over the pages again, "was a very unpleasant person. There is no use pretending that I'm sorry he's dead. I'm not. I do wish though that he had met his death in a more conventional manner."

He laid the manuscript down and looked at me with a quizzical expression on his face.

"I brought you a visitor," he said. "George Hathaway wanted to see how you were getting along. Shall I send him up? You don't have to see him if you don't want to. I can tell him that you aren't well enough to be having visitors."

"Send him up by all means," I said promptly. "I'll be glad to see him. We're companions of the hunt, you know. Rabbit hunting. He's very good at it."

"All right. Don't let him stay long, though. You need rest. He'll have to walk back. I have another patient I must see."

I heard the doctor's car leave as George stomped heavily up the stairs followed by Henry. He came into the room with a sheepish grin on his face.

"Morning," he said awkwardly. "I wanted to see how you was. And I wanted to tell you something."

"Sit down," I said, motioning toward a chair. He perched himself gingerly on its edge. Henry seated himself on Joan's bed.

"I'm all right," I told him. "The doctor says I can get out of bed in a few days."

"I knew a man once that was bit by a snake," he said. "But he died."

"That's nice. Tell me about it."

"Well, he walked out barefoot at night. Went out in the garden to go to the outhouse. Stepped right on it, he did. He yelled and ran back to the house. The snake got away."

"What did you say he stepped on?" Henry murmured.

"The snake," Hathaway said, turning toward him. "It bit him right on the foot. He was dead before morning. Swelled up something awful, too."

"That's comforting. But I don't think I'm going to die. At least the doctor tells me I won't."

"Oh, your bite ain't nothing. You had a boot on. By rights you shouldn't have got the poison at all."

"Tell Mr. Whitby what you told me," Henry said to him.

"About the doctor, you mean?"

Henry nodded.

"Well, he's scared. I think he's afraid of getting murdered. And I sort of suspect he knows who killed his brother and he's afraid that whoever it is is going to try to kill him, too."

"What makes you think so?"

"Every night he goes around and locks up the house. We ain't never locked it up before. And he took Howard's shotgun up in his room."

"Has he said anything?"

"No, he ain't said a word to me."

"Anything else?"

"He don't sleep in Howard's room. He took a room upstairs. A little room that used to be his when he was a boy. He put a bolt on the door, too. A heavy iron bolt from the barn. And he's going to have a telephone put up there. I heard him talk to the company to arrange it."

"He seems all right," I said dubiously. "He was cheerful enough this morning."

"He's always cheerful," Hathaway said. "He ain't like Howard at all. Howard used to go for days without saying a word to me."

"Is there anything we can do?"

"I'd like to see that murderer caught," he said earnestly.

"So would I," Henry told him. "You just sit tight and we'll get him."

Hathaway got up to go.

"Maybe you'd like to have some sweet corn," he said. "I got some with black kernels. It looks funny but it's real good."

"Thanks," I said. "I do like corn. We have only the common varieties."

"I'll bring some over tomorrow."

When he had gone I looked at Henry who just sat and grinned at me.

"Well," I said peevishly, "why don't you do something about it? It looks as if we might have another murder on our hands unless this case is solved quickly. What are you grinning about?"

"Doesn't it seem a bit strange to you that the doctor should bring Hathaway here to tell us how frightened his employer is?"

"He didn't. George came here ostensibly to find out how I was."

"Ostensibly is the right word. The doctor must have known that Hathaway would talk about his actions."

"Why should he want us to know?"

"You guess."

"Maybe he wants you to realize that he is in danger. That the murderer may strike at him now that his brother is dead."

Henry grunted. "I shouldn't be at all surprised. The doctor is candidate number one for death in this village now, if I have this case figured out right."

"Well, why don't you do something about it?" I said impatiently.

"What do you think I've been running around for? I am doing something about it. But I can't do anything yet. The case isn't ripe. It's got to come to a head of its own accord."

Helen brought my lunch up to me. She sat down on Joan's bed and kept me company while I ate. Tinkel, who had been put out of the room several times by force, stuck her head inquiringly through the doorway.

"How's the work going?" I asked. "Are you getting all those slides mounted?"

She nodded. "Don't you worry about it. We'll have more slides made up than you can use. Take your mind off the subject and relax. You're supposed to be sick and you're crazy to try to keep on writing those technical descriptions now."

Tinkel began to edge softly into the room.

"I understand that you and Henry were alone here last night."

"If you call having Emma around as a chaperone being alone," she said with a grin, "She went to bed at nine o'clock, though."

"I suppose Henry spent the entire evening talking about the murder?"

"No, as a matter of fact he didn't say a word about it. He told me all about his childhood."

"That's bad," I said frowning. "When a man tells a woman about his childhood it means that he is getting seriously sentimental."

"What's wrong about that?" she asked placidly. "I told him all about my childhood, too. I was very unhappy because we were always moving around from place to place and Marjorie and I never had any friends."

"Neither of you seems to be suffering very much from that any more."

"No," she said slowly, "but I'm getting worried about Marjorie. I'm afraid she's going to marry a broker. All he ever talks about is steel and horses. I like horses but somehow I can't get interested in steel. Besides, I hate the prospect of being my own sister's poor relation."

Suddenly Tinkel made a dash for the bed. Helen grabbed her, spanked her soundly, and thrust her out of the room. She sat down in the hallway looking very unhappy.

"Tell me," I said when things had quieted down, "how did you ever become interested in biology—especially such a recondite part of it as mycology?"

"I was always interested in biology," she said earnestly. "I like to see things grow. Flowers and kittens and babies—oh, anything."

"But mycology?"

"You were the reason for that," she said blushing slightly. "The other profs were—well, you know what old Jennings is like. And as for that silly Mr. Brookings—I never could stand him. He whistles every time he comes to an S."

"I thought you were really interested in the subject," I said sternly.

"Oh, I am! I like microscope work. It's like looking into another world. I'd take up bacteriology too if there was a decent course in it at school."

"I suppose that what will actually happen is that you'll get married and be so busy with babies and diapers and things that you won't have time for such trifles as scientific research."

"What's wrong with babies?"

Joan came up the stairs and into the room before I could answer.

"Mr. Marigold is here," she said briefly. "You're getting to be awfully popular. I asked him to stay for lunch."

"I want to meet him," Helen whispered. "Henry has told me all about him. Let me stay and watch."

"Send him up," I said grandly to Joan. "Maybe he has some amusing stories to tell about torture in Afghanistan. I don't think he's covered that yet."

Marigold came upstairs with a tread that was surprisingly light for a person of his build. He was carrying a bunch of white roses.

"I brought you some flowers," he said. "They're always so nice in a sickroom."

Marigold nodded casually to Helen upon being introduced and sat down on the chair near the bed.

"Well, how is the invalid this morning? It must be quite an experience to be bitten by a poisonous snake. Of course these North American pit vipers can't be compared with tropical thanatophidia for venomousness but I suppose that even a copperhead can give one a nasty turn."

"People do die regularly from copperhead bites," I protested. "They're mighty damned poisonous. I was lucky enough to be bitten through my boot."

"Of course, of course," said Marigold soothingly. "I wasn't trying to belittle your danger. I just wanted to point out that you were lucky it wasn't a cobra. I came within an ace of being bitten by a cobra once."

"How did that happen?"

"Oh, an Indian snake charmer was toying with a couple of them. I was sure that the snakes had been defanged. I was wrong." He shrugged his shoulders. "We can't always be right, can we?" he said with a deprecating smile.

Suddenly his face became serious.

"I saw Doctor Stanton this morning. He stopped to talk with me for a moment as he passed my house on his way to visit you. I'm worried about him. Did you notice the way he acts? He is afraid of something. I can see death in his eyes!"

"Can you?" I said politely. "I have never had any experience seeing death in people's eyes so I wouldn't know what to look for."

"Mark my words," Marigold said. "I'm not joking. That man is staring death in the face and he knows it."

CHAPTER XXI
THE POLICE TAKE ACTION

Henry soon became fast friends with the men at the state police headquarters in Fammelton. He played poker with them in their idle hours with results that were disastrous to his pocketbook but in this way he was able to be on the spot when the next development in the Stanton affair took place.

He came back to the house in low spirits one evening. I had been moved downstairs and was stretched out in a steamer chair on the wide back porch. Joan and Helen were playing checkers—which meant that we had to have a light—and a light on a summer evening attracts swarms of insects that drum annoyingly on the porch screens. Henry dropped into a chair without a word of greeting and tapped nervously on its arm with a cigarette that he had just drawn out of a fresh pack. The girls looked up questioningly.

"What's up?" I asked in a casual tone.

"The police think they have solved the case," he said slowly.

We clamored for particulars.

With exasperating deliberation he began to search his pockets for a match. Helen quickly proffered her lighted cigarette, and he lit his from it, drawing in the smoke and exhaling it in a dense cloud.

"Chases the mosquitoes away," he said apologetically.

"There aren't any mosquitoes," Joan told him coldly. Mosquitoes are a sore point with us. We don't have any, but sometimes we find it difficult to convince our guests.

"Of course not," he agreed. "They don't like smoke."

"There never—"

"Are we going to talk about mosquitoes or murder?" asked Helen. "Because if it's going to be mosquitoes, I'd rather go back to checkers. I'm winning this game."

"Let's talk about murder then," Joan said.

"Okay," said Henry obediently. "We'll talk about murder. I'm not sure though, that what I have to tell you about is really murder. The whole thing seems a bit fishy to me."

"Never mind what you think," Helen said. "Begin at the beginning and tell us what happened."

I leaned over and snapped off the porch light. Henry's cigarette gleamed for a moment in the darkness, and then he stamped it out and began in earnest.

"I reached Fammelton just as the morning mail was delivered to headquarters. There was a letter there, postmarked Calverton. It was unsigned—one of those 'From a Friend' things. I'm convinced that Mrs. Morton sent it—it had all the earmarks of her handiwork—but that's neither here nor there. It was very short. It merely said: *Ask Mary Morgan why she ran out of the entrance to the Stanton tenant farm shortly after eight o'clock on the night Howard Stanton was killed. Ask her why she was crying.*

"Macready, Anderson, Hamilton, and I piled into the police car and drove up here to Brookdale in twenty-eight minutes flat."

"Why did they let you in on it?" I demanded.

"I happened to be paying the captain thirty-seven dollars for a poker debt just as the letter arrived. It was the least he could do," Henry answered with a chuckle.

"Evidently the ability to play poker badly is one of the chief requisites of an amateur detective," I observed caustically.

Henry ignored me and went on.

"Bill Morgan and his father were out haying when we drove up to the Morgan farm. That was a lucky break, for it gave the captain a chance to question Mary alone.

"'Mrs. Morgan,' he began very solemnly, 'I have a witness who saw everything that took place between you and Howard Stanton at his tenant farm on the night he was murdered. The witness is willing to testify in court—I would advise you to tell me yourself, in your own words, just what happened that night although I must warn you that anything you say may be used against you.'"

"What a dirty, trick!" Helen cried. "He didn't know anything at all!"

"Of course not," Henry said quickly. "He was just trying to scare her and he did. She turned white and cried out: 'He didn't do it! He didn't do it! Someone else had already killed Howard!' And then she sat down on the edge of the porch and began to cry.

"Macready motioned to Anderson to go and get her husband. He brought Bill Morgan in about ten minutes later. His father was with him, Anderson hadn't told them anything, of course, but when Bill saw his wife he knew that something was up. I saw him look around for a minute and I could imagine what he was thinking about, but the sight of the automatics in the open holsters of the troopers must have discouraged any idea of escape. He said nothing at all but just stood there looking at his wife.

"'Your wife has told us about your visit to Howard Stanton's tenant farm last Tuesday evening. Don't you think you had better tell us the whole story?' the captain said. 'It's for your own benefit.'

"Morgan ran his tongue over his dry lips and stood shifting his weight from foot to foot. 'What did you tell them?' he asked her finally.

"She looked up suddenly and said, 'I told them you didn't do it. I told them that when you got there Howard was already dead!'

"'That's all?' he asked quietly.

"She nodded.

"'Well, that's true enough,' he said defiantly. 'He was dead and hanging from a tree. If he hadn't been, I'd have killed him.'

"Macready took off his cap and ran his handkerchief around the wet headband.

"'You'd better tell us the whole story, son,' he said to Morgan."

"I think that's a shame," Joan said indignantly. "I'm sure it's not legal. Bill should have insisted on getting a lawyer before he said anything."

Henry lit a fresh cigarette and said: "Well, maybe, but anyway we all walked around the house to the shady side and sat down on the lawn. It was like a social visit. Quite informal—just the guns of the police to remind us of the business on hand.

"Bill Morgan pulled up a white clover blossom and began to chew it. His wife sat next to him and he placed his big hand over one of hers. His father squatted down on his haunches and didn't say a word.

"'Well,' Morgan began in a voice as toneless as though he were discussing the hay crop, 'last fall Mary helped Mrs. Denner do a lot of canning. She was supposed to get paid for it—twelve dollars it was—but Howard stalled her off all winter. She went out for a walk last Tuesday evening and she saw George Hathaway drive Howard's hay wagon out of the tenant farm and turn up the road toward Calverton. She saw Howard himself in the field so she naturally went after him to get the money he rightfully owed her. He didn't want to give it to her—said that it ought to come out of Mrs. Denner's household expenses. Well, she knew there wasn't any money for household expenses. One word led to another and she finally called him an old skinflint—or something like that. He hit her—slapped her really, I suppose. Anyway, she fell down. And she's expecting. He didn't know that, of course, but he hadn't ought to have hit a woman anyway. She started to cry and ran home. She didn't tell me about it right off but when she did I started up to go after him. I'd have killed him right enough, I guess, but somebody else must have got there first. I don't know who it was but if I did, I'd like to shake his hand. Howard Stanton was ripe for killing for a good while and he only got what was coming to him, but I didn't do it.'

"We were all silent for a moment. I believed every word that Morgan had said but I knew he'd have a hard time proving his innocence.

"At last the captain asked: 'And you didn't see anyone at all? Didn't hear anything?'

"Morgan shook his head. 'I wouldn't have,' he said simply. 'I was too mad. I don't even remember walking up there. It was dark by the time I got there. When I went across the bridge I ran into Howard's body. I had to strike a match to see what it was. Then I ran all the way home.'

"'Why didn't you report the murder?'

"'I was afraid to,' Morgan said. 'I thought it might be blamed on me. I knew Howard was dead. There was blood all over him. And I knew somebody else would find the body as soon as he was missed, so it seemed smart for me to mind my own business right then.'

"'Do you know what time it was when you got back to your house?'

"'It was just a couple of minutes after nine, new time. I looked at the kitchen clock when I came in.'

"'And how long do you think it took you to run home?'

"'I ran fast,' he said, smiling feebly. 'I must have done it in less than five minutes.'

"'I'm afraid we'll have to take you down to Fammelton,' the captain said. Then he turned to Morgan's wife. 'Don't you worry about it,' he told her. 'Everything will be all right.'

"Mary Morgan said nothing but just sat there white-faced, clutching her husband's arm.

"Finally Morgan got to his feet.

"'What about this witness of yours who claims to know so much about it?' he asked.

"'I'll send you on to Fammelton in the police car,' the captain told him. 'And I'll stay here in Brookdale and round up the witness for you.'

"Macready then went over to Hamilton and whispered some instructions to him. Hamilton and Anderson put their prisoner between them in the front seat and drove off.

"Just as they were going Bill Morgan's mother showed up. We had quite a time with her. I can tell you that I was glad to get away.

"I had told the captain of my suspicions that Mrs. Morton was the author of the letter, so we went over to see her. She wrote it, all right. The sight of a uniform and a gold badge brought the story out of her quickly. It was very simple really. She had been driving toward Calverton that night and she saw Mary come out of the Stanton tenant farm entrance. Mary was crying but the incident became important to that old busybody, of course, only after she heard of Stanton's murder."

"If anything happens to Bill, Ramsey Morgan will kill that woman," Joan said fiercely. "And no jury would hold him for it, either."

"Morgan doesn't know that Mrs. Morton is the one who squealed," Henry said. "Nobody does. It's a police secret and I want you all to keep it quiet. There'll be hell to pay if it should get out."

"She'll have to testify in court," I objected. "Everybody will know then."

"When she is brought to the witness stand and makes her story public, that will be another matter," Henry said. "But meanwhile I'm the only one outside the police force who knows about it, and it would be awfully unpleasant for me if the news got out. I have a good in with the police now but they'd be off me for life if they found out I'd been talking. Keep it quiet, please."

"That boy is being railroaded into the chair," Joan said hotly. "The whole thing is just too rotten."

"The captain is far from convinced that Bill Morgan is the actual slayer," Henry told her, "but I'm afraid the police want to hang the crime on someone. I went back to Fammelton with him when the police car returned. The news had already been made public. I suppose even the city papers will play it up tomorrow."

"It seems pretty raw, though," Helen said thoughtfully.

"Don't worry," Henry said. "He won't be railroaded. Not while I'm here. Remember, I'm working on this case."

Joan snorted. "If I were in Bill Morgan's shoes, I'd mortgage the old homestead and go out and hire a real detective."

CHAPTER XXII
THE UNHAPPY BRIDE

After a few days I found that my enforced invalidism was not particularly conducive to work. I had started with a burst of renewed enthusiasm at the actual business of writing the text of my book but after the first few days I discovered how extraordinarily pleasant it was just to lie in the sun stretched out on a steamer chair and watch the great white cloud masses drift over the mountain. I had always worked hard—I now began to discover the sybaritic pleasures of idleness.

Joan and Helen, of course, had to go on with their work but I shirked shamelessly and was excused for it because I was supposed to be recuperating. Perhaps some of the snake's venom had tempered my blood with something that induced this feeling of lassitude. At any rate, I welcomed even Emma's efforts at conversation because they permitted me to put off the mental effort that my work required.

Nothing delighted Emma more than talking about her girlhood. There was a great deal of the child in her. Sometimes she borrowed books from us which she would slowly and laboriously read. She always picked those with easy words and short sentences. Aesop's and La Fontaine's *Fables, Alice in Wonderland,* and *Pilgrim's Progress* were her particular favorites.

She had spent the first sixteen years of her life in an old stone house that stood halfway up a hill not far beyond the village. The house had passed into the hands of city people but Emma always looked upon it as her own home. She would talk to me for hours about her father who had been a mighty hunter and a redoubtable eel-fisherman, and she told me about her brother who had saved someone on the mountain from falling over the edge of a "prepuce." But most of all she talked about the village people.

Naturally enough, I was particularly interested in the Morgan family. Bill Morgan was being held for the grand jury and the county had already become divided into two factions over the matter of his probable guilt.

Emma presented me with a complete résumé of his family history which seemed to me to differ in no unusual way from the history of any other local family. Bill's great grandfather on his paternal side had distinguished himself as a soldier in the Civil War. His father had been a volunteer in the Spanish-American War, but Bill himself had been too young to do anything about making the world safe for democracy. He had married Mary about three years ago. She had been taken into his father's household from an orphanage. Emma let her fancy have free reign about the girl's possible origin but I firmly refused to take any stock in her mysterious hints.

Mary Morgan took her husband's arrest very hard. Emma told me that Mary's mother-in-law, who had always seemed to me to be an unusually kind and pleasant person, was in reality a martinet who had exploited Mary ruthlessly. She had never approved of her son's marriage and she now blamed his arrest on his wife. The little house where the young couple lived had formerly been a wagon shed. Bill Morgan had fixed it up as a house for his bride and it was furnished with pathetic odds and ends that had been discarded from his parents' home. I could imagine how the poor girl felt, living there all alone, waiting for her child to be born, with her husband in jail and her mother-in-law accusing her daily of having sent him there.

She seldom left the house, Emma said. She was afraid to face her neighbors and she no longer even went to see Edgar Harmon, who had been a very special friend of hers.

I had heard by way of Miss Harvey and Emma that Harmon was in even poorer health than usual. He had had a fainting spell. Miss Harvey had revived him with smelling salts, and when he came to, she wanted to call a doctor. He had forbidden her to do so, saying that it was useless—the sooner he died the better it would be for everyone, himself included.

I determined to visit him. I wanted to see how he was, and I wanted to talk to him about Mary Morgan. Since I was now permitted to hobble around with a cane, I had Henry drive me to his house one afternoon. The shades in the invalid's room were pulled down to keep out the heat but even in the dim light I could see that he was pale and his hand shook when he extended it to me. Ordinarily he was glad to see me but now he was morose and gloomy. When I brought up the subject of Bill Morgan's arrest he became quite vehement in his denunciation of the police. The boy was innocent, he said, and he was certain that no jury of Hampton County men would ever convict him.

I spoke to him about Mary.

"I wish she would come to see me," he said. "I can't go to her and I know she's in trouble. She used to come over here when she was a little girl. Mrs. Morgan is a typical puritan. She makes a virtue of work and she always expected that poor little kid to like washing dishes and feeding pigs."

"Bill Morgan will be out of jail in a short while now," I told him, "and then everything will be all right. Mary will have her husband back, a baby to take care of, and some day they'll inherit the farm and the big house."

"She deserves it," he said shortly. "She's had a hell of a life."

To ease the situation, I tried rather ineptly to lead Harmon into a discussion of the Spanish-American War and

the men from our village who had taken part in it. He
was not very eager to talk about it, however. Harmon, I
knew, had been awarded some kind of medal for his services on San Juan Hill, but I suppose that any sensitive
mind can hardly dwell with fond recollection on military
honors which are won only at the cost of human lives and
suffering. He had become an avowed pacifist and held that
the United States with its vast area was practically im-
pregnable to any foreign invasion. He began to talk about
the munitions racket and he spoke bitterly of the men
who had profiteered in spoiled beef during the campaign
of '98.

"There seems to be no limit to human vileness," he
said slowly. "Deceit, betrayal, wanton cruelty—all these
are characteristic only of man. Animals kill swiftly and for
food. It seems that our much-vaunted human intelligence
brings with it a calculating selfishness that no dumb tiger
or wolf would be clever enough to imagine. Nor do we
improve with time and education. Terror spreads across
the world and violence grows more common every day.
Sometimes I dread reading the daily paper with its stories
of court-martials and purges, injustice and brutal repres-
sion." He ceased speaking and reached for a cigarette.

Henry, who had been wrapped up in his own thoughts,
suddenly jumped up and ran across the room to offer him
a light. I could see Harmon's big troubled eyes stare un-
waveringly into the flame.

The close, darkened room with its still figure lying in
bed began to grow oppressive. As we got up to go I noticed a slight movement in the far corner of the room. It
was Emmett. He had been there all the time but I hadn't
noticed his presence. I was glad to get out into the sunshine again. I had to stop at Joe Fammel's store to tell an
inquisitive audience all about the snake bite. Then Henry
drove me back to the house.

I wondered what was going to become of Bill Morgan.
When we reached the house I found that the first step

in the implacable proceedings of the law had been taken against him. Emma told us that Anderson had left a message for Henry. It said very simply that Bill Morgan had been indicted by the grand jury for murder in the first degree.

As usual we discussed the latest developments in the case at the house that night. Henry had carefully examined Bill Morgan's car which now stood idle in his father's barn.

"It can't be the car that was on the Rocky Hill road that night," he said. "Bill's car is an old Ford and we know that the murderer's car was larger than a Ford. The tire mark wasn't very clear but it certainly was made by a wider tire than a three and one-half inch one. The V-shaped mark I've already discounted, of course. Any murderer in his right mind would have changed tires afterward. Bill's tires are old ones that have been on the rims a long while. They'll have a hard time trying to link up his car with the murder of Whiskey Joe, all right. The whole trouble is that he's indicted only for the Stanton murder, and I will frankly admit that I don't see a ghost of an alibi for him on that."

"Speaking of alibis," I said, "what have you been doing about the alibis of the Strongs, the Mortons, *et al?*"

"I can't get anything at all on the Strongs. I've stopped three times at their service station to buy gas or oil that I didn't need so I could start a conversation but all I could get out of that guy was 'Yep' and 'Nope.'"

"He just doesn't like to talk," Joan said. "I saw him at a store in Calverton a few days ago. He had a long list of things to buy for his wife so he just handed the list to the storekeeper, waited until everything was ready, paid the bill, and walked out of the store without a word."

"He'd make a wonderful witness," Henry said. "He'd drive Max Steuer nuts in ten minutes."

"Well, what about the Mortons?" I asked. "It's no trouble getting Henry Morton to talk. He loves it."

"Did he ever tell you how he saved Howard Stanton's life? It was at the battle of San Juan Hill."

"Yes, yes. I've heard all that and it doesn't mean a thing. Did you get anything useful from him?"

"Well, I don't know what you'd call useful," Henry said judiciously. "I invested a quart of applejack and four hours of my young life in trying to learn something about Mr. Morton. I found out all about his unhappy childhood; I am now an expert on army life during the Spanish-American War; I listened to his tale of woe about his wife, and I am fully acquainted with Mr. Morton's views on politics, religion, education, and sex. But I don't quite see how any of the information I obtained ties up with either murder."

"Did it occur to you to ask him where he was on the night Stanton was murdered?"

"Sure. He told me he was sitting on the back porch with Mrs. Morton until nine o'clock. Then they went to bed. They've been doing that every night for thirty-five years."

"In winter, too?" Helen asked.

"They vary it in winter," he explained. "In winter they sit in the kitchen and go to bed at eight o'clock."

"Wait a minute," I said quickly. "Mrs. Morton told the police that she saw Mary Morgan at eight o'clock while she was on her way to Calverton that night. There's something phony about this."

"Sure there is," Henry admitted cheerfully. "Somebody's lying. I know that. Morton told me that story before his wife spilled the beans to the police, of course."

"Nice people."

"Henry Morton's not so bad. He's just been pushed around a lot."

"I wonder where he really was that night."

"He was in Calverton," Henry said. "I found that out. He'd been playing pool with some of the creamery boys. His wife drove up to bring him home."

"Why do you suppose he lied then?"

Henry shrugged his shoulders. "Just dumb, I guess. Thought he could get away with it."

"What time did Mrs. Morton tell the police she came home that night?"

"Eleven o'clock. And she admitted bringing her husband home with her."

"What time did she really leave Calverton?"

"I can't prove what time she actually left but she dragged her husband out of that pool game well before nine o'clock."

"Maybe they went somewhere else in Calverton," Helen suggested.

"Perhaps. I don't know. It'll all come out when they cross-examine the lady, I suppose."

Henry began to drum on the arm of his chair with his fingers.

"Have you seen any more of my dear friend, Mr. Marigold?" I asked.

"I've had several chitchats with him over the tea table. I told him about some photographs of murder, suicide, and rape cases that I saw in an exhibition of police-department photos at the Academy of Medicine, and he showed me some pictures he had gotten from a friend in China. We had a wonderful time. Did you ever hear of the method of killing known as 'Lin sen'? It might be described as the death of a thousand cuts. It's quite a stunt. They take a sharp knife and start making ribbons—"

"Never mind," I said hastily. "Did you learn anything about his alibi?"

"Alibi? Oh yes, alibi," Henry grinned. "Well, you remember he told the police that he had been home reading during the time both murders took place? I asked him how it was that there was no light in his house on the night Whiskey Joe was killed. We passed there several times that night, and I noticed that the house was dark."

"Did you? I didn't pay any attention to it," I said in some surprise. "What did he have to say?"

"He was rather confused for a moment and then he said that we wouldn't have seen any light because he always reads with a little reading-light gadget that he clips on the book so that it only illuminates the page."

"More likely he was attending a witches' sabbat," Joan suggested.

"Why don't you take me to visit Mr. Marigold's house?" Helen said to Henry. "It must be a fascinating place. Has he got an altar for the Black Mass?"

"I'll take you there tomorrow and we'll look," Henry said promptly.

"I want to see this famous cat of his, too. I love Siamese cats. They're so slinky."

"You're lucky if you see it," Henry said. "I never have. I think it must be his familiar. He's just the sort of person who would have a familiar. It's queer that he calls it Herman. It's such an unaesthetic name. Grimalkin or Ilemanzar would be so much more appropriate."

The next day promised to be unusually warm. I was up early and went down to the brook discreetly clad in bathing trunks, which was a good thing, for in about five minutes Joan and Helen came down to bathe.

Helen came out of the water glistening like a wet seal. She climbed up on the rock I was sitting on and took off her rubber bathing cap. Her long blonde hair tumbled down over her shoulders.

"Henry is awfully worried," she said. "About Bill Morgan."

"Damn Henry," I said grumpily. "All I hear about around here is Henry and his confounded murders. Now he's got you going, too. I used to think you had the makings of a good biologist in you. Besides, you're much too pretty to be a murder fan. Murder fans are frustrated people like Henry. He's frustrated because he hates his job and has no other interest in life—except mystery stories."

"Henry's not so bad. I rather like him."

"Oh, you do, do you? Well—"

Joan stood up and waded over to the rock.

"What's the matter with Henry?"

"He's frustrated. I was just telling Helen about it."

"What Henry needs," said Joan positively, "is a wife and a home and children. He needs somebody to look after him. He spends all his money on cameras and wine and—"

"Don't worry about Henry," I said. "He's a very fortunate bachelor. He might better spend his money on cameras than on buying shoes for some female. Cameras are much more useful and they're certainly a whole lot more interesting than expensive and trivial feminine footwear."

"My husband," said Joan in a glacial voice, "is making indirect and ill-bred references to the fact that I paid fifteen dollars for a pair of shoes last fall. Last fall, mind you! Why, Henry spent seventy-five dollars for a second-hand lens! He told me so."

"So what? Why shouldn't Henry spend seven! five dollars for a lens if he wants to? He has no wife to support. And from what he tells me," I said darkly, "he doesn't need one. You know the old proverb about keeping a cow. He'd be a fool to get married."

Helen giggled. "Why tell me? I have no evil designs on Henry."

I glared at Joan. She was combing her hair and she looked at me with a blandly innocent expression on her face.

"Let's eat breakfast," I said disgustedly.

It was late when we finished eating but there was still no sign of Henry and Emma. Finally the two girls started to wash the dishes. They had hardly begun when we heard the honking of our own car's horn. I ran outside. Henry was coming up the road at breakneck speed. He brought the car to stop with shrieking brakes. Emma's face was portentous of disaster.

"Mary Morgan's killed herself," she said abruptly. "She hanged herself in Ramsey's barn early this morning."

CHAPTER XXIII
TONIGHT IS THE NIGHT!

As I remember that next morning the thing that comes back most vividly to my mind is the extraordinary number of flies that were in the house. They kept buzzing around, and even a determined campaign waged against them with Flit-gun and swatter hardly seemed to decrease their number appreciably.

The air was sultry and there was a light mist that hung in the air and obscured the sun. Everything was sticky and everyone was uncomfortable. Even Tinkel, who loves the heat, was lying on the floor panting and occasionally snapping at one of the horde of houseflies.

Henry let Emma tell the story of Mary Morgan's suicide. Miss Harvey, who had made an early morning visit to Joe Fammel's store, had brought them the news. They had immediately gone to the Morgan farm.

"They'd taken her into the house before we got there," Emma said. "Into the big house. I went into the wagon shed where Mary lived. She had washed up the breakfast dishes and made the bed." Emma sloshed water angrily around the sink. "She'd even fed the pigs." Her voice broke.

"Did she leave a note of any kind?" I asked Henry.

"Apparently not. They didn't find any."

"Maybe it wasn't suicide," I said pointedly.

Henry shook his head. "I thought of that. But I went into the barn. She had pulled a wagon under the big center beam, and she had stood up on the driving seat."

"So?"

"Well," he said slowly, "it wasn't murder. There was a comb there, and a box of powder. She had combed her hair first, and powdered her face."

"Women certainly are queer," I said. "I wonder if she knew what the face of a hanged person looks like?"

"Probably not. I hope not, anyway. I saw her face as she lay on the bed in her mother-in-law's house. The powder was all streaked with tears."

Emma began to sob.

I motioned to Henry to go outside with me. We sat down on the lawn behind the house. We were silent for a long while.

"Why do you think she did it?" I asked.

He shrugged his shoulders. "The poor kid probably thought that her husband was really guilty. After all, she had no way of knowing for sure. He had gone up to see Stanton that night while he was in a murderous rage. And then Stanton was found dead. Her mother-in-law probably helped to drive her over the edge, too."

"Well? What's next?"

"Plenty," he said. "If I'm any good at guessing, this case is going to break wide open in the next twenty-four hours."

"Why don't you tell me what your theory is then? It's really very childish of you to act like a conventional detective-story sleuth now."

"I can't tell you yet," Henry said seriously. "I really can't. When it's all over you'll understand why."

"Well, I think you're being pretty silly, anyway. Tell me if there are any new developments, at least. How about Mrs. Morton? How is she taking it?"

Henry twisted around to look back at the porch so he could make sure Emma was not within hearing distance.

"I think Mrs. Morton has cleared out," he said.

"What do you mean?"

"I had to take Emma back to her house before we drove up here. She forgot her work shoes. I saw the Morton car come out of the driveway of their house. Mrs. and Mr. Morton were both in it, all dressed up in their best clothes. They headed west in a hurry. I'd say that the lady is going to make a sudden visit to some relative in another part of the state. And I don't think she'll be back in a hurry."

"Maybe they're both making a getaway! Henry Morton might be the murderer," I said excitedly.

"They won't get far," Henry grinned. "I took the license number and gave it to Anderson. He was at the Morgan house, of course."

"Did he go after them?"

"He went to Fammel's and phoned for a motorcycle cop to pick them up on the main road. He won't make a pinch, of course. Just follow them to see where they go."

"They'll notice the motorcycle," I objected. "The cop can't keep out of sight all the time."

"He doesn't have to. I want them to realize that they're being followed," Henry said maliciously. "I'd like to see the old woman's face when she catches wise to the fact that a cop is tailing her car. Maybe what she'll go through then will help to make up a little for the trouble she's caused."

Henry stretched himself out on the grass and looked up at the sky. Two turkey buzzards were circling around the western end of the mountain. Everything was unnaturally still. There was no trace of a breeze and birds and insects were curiously silent. Only the rushing sound of the brook came to us.

"I feel terrible about Mary," Henry said finally. "It was all so unnecessary. I'm certainly glad I had no part in it. In fact it would never have happened if those dumb cops had listened to me. Well, they're listening now, all right— Anderson is, anyway."

"What have you got up your sleeve?"

"You'll see. Tonight's the night. It must happen tonight. I hope everything goes off all right though, or there's going to be still more business for the undertaker in this town."

I looked up in alarm.

"Don't worry. I've got everything fixed," he said. There was a pause. Then he added: "I hope."

"Anderson is going to help you?"

He nodded. "Yes. He's the only one, though. I can't persuade that thick-headed police captain that I'm right. He's more certain than ever now that Bill Morgan is guilty. Says that Mary's suicide proves it. Anderson's willing to take a chance with me, though. We'll handle it alone. I'll have my .45 Colt with me. And Anderson has a gun, of course."

"Let me go with you," I begged. "I was in at the very start of this affair and I'd like to see the finish. Besides, I might be useful. There are only two of you. . . ."

"I'll talk to Anderson," Henry promised. "It might be a good thing to have you along. I may want to call on you to speak your little piece if things turn out the way I think they're going to."

I could no longer pretend even to myself that I was uninterested in the case. The suicide of Mary Morgan had made me realize that.

I went to the village with Henry. Joe Fammel, David Hamlin, and Cal Smith were seated on the bench in front of the store.

Dave Hamlin looked at Henry for a moment with a curious expression on his face. Then he said: "Young man, you didn't have anything to do with Bill Morgan's arrest, did you?"

"No, certainly not," Henry said a trifle irritably, I thought. "I told the police they were making a mistake holding him. Bill Morgan didn't kill Stanton. I'm as sure of that as anyone can be. Furthermore I hope to be able to prove it—in a very short time, too."

"I'm glad of that, son," Hamlin said laconically. "Some people around here have been saying it was you as caused Bill's arrest. It was somebody. We know that."

"Well, it wasn't me," Henry said. "I've visited Bill Morgan in the jail and talked with him. He knows I'm working to get him out."

"I told 'em you wasn't the one," Cal Smith said. "I told 'em how you started the idea of raising money so we could bury Whiskey Joe proper. I said you were all right."

"Thanks," Henry said briefly. He turned to Joe Fammel. "I'd like to get some cigarettes."

Joe brought him a pack. Henry seemed quite eager to get away. He went to the car, mumbling something about being in a hurry.

As we drove away I asked him what was the matter.

"I was afraid that guy was going to ask me if I knew who did tip the police off. I'd have been in a tough spot then."

"You'll probably get lynched before you're through with this affair. Where are you going now?"

"I don't know," he said, slowing up the car. "I just wanted to get away from that bunch at the store."

"Dave Hamlin was out looking for trouble, all right. He's a good friend of the Morgans', you know."

"I hope he believed what I told him."

"You'd better lay low until he has a chance to spread the story around that you had nothing to do with Morgan's arrest. By the way, you didn't tell me that you talked with him in jail. What did he have to say?"

Henry stopped the car by the side of the road and left the engine running.

"He told me all over again the story of how he found Howard Stanton's body. Then, he told me something else. Asked me not to pass it on to the police."

"What was it?"

"Well, on his way to the Stanton farm he saw a car coming down the road toward him. He didn't want to be seen so he ducked into the bushes. He recognized the car. It was the Mortons' old Buick. There were two people in it—a man who was driving and a woman in the front seat alongside him. He thought it was Mr. and Mrs. Morton but he couldn't swear to it. It was pretty dark by then, of course."

"So the old harpy was lying when she said they left Calverton at eleven o'clock?"

"Seems that way. I couldn't fix the exact time she took her husband out of that pool game but it's possible that they had enough time to kill Stanton and clear out before Bill Morgan got there, if that's what you're thinking."

Henry let in the clutch, shifted into first, and started the car moving again.

"I asked Anderson to come up to your house for lunch. I hope you won't mind. He's going to stick around all day just to be handy. I don't expect anything to happen before dark but I thought Anderson ought to be here anyway."

Joan, Helen, and Emma had evidently drained the possibilities of Mary Morgan's suicide to their emotional dregs. At any rate, they had ceased discussing the matter and the atmosphere was slightly more cheerful when we returned. The flies were still there though. We had lunch on the screened porch. Anderson didn't show up until we were almost through eating.

"What news from the front, Courier?" Henry asked as Anderson strode out on the porch.

"All quiet, General. I thought you were coming back to the Morgan farm, though."

"I thought so too, but I seem to have worn out my welcome in Brookdale." Henry told the trooper of our conversation with Dave Hamlin.

Helen was alarmed. "I don't think you ought to sleep at Emma's house tonight," she said. "He can stay here, can't he?" she asked Joan. "He could sleep on the parlor couch."

"Of course," Joan said. "He can stay here any time he wants to. He knows that."

"Thanks," Henry said grinning, with a warm look at Helen. "I may be out late, though. Let's go down to the brook and cool off meanwhile."

Anderson was a bit dubious about the advisability of taking off his heavy uniform and puttees.

"I'm on duty, you know," he said. "If the captain should come up here and find me playing around, I'd be in a hell of a fix."

"Well, come down and sit on a rock so you can keep an eye on us," Henry told him. "Then you'll be on duty and anyway, it's cooler down there. We need you. The murderer might pop out of the woods with a rope in one hand and a stone in the other. As taxpayers we're entitled to a little police protection."

We changed, and went down to bathe. The sunlight kept slowly fading until the sky was completely overcast. It was evident that we were going to have rain before the day was through.

After a few minutes in the water, Henry and I joined Anderson who was sitting on a big rock, smoking cigarettes that he rolled himself. The girls continued to swim idly in the dark waters of the pool.

"How did you ever get into police work?" I asked Anderson. "I've often wondered how it happens."

"My uncle was a cop," he said. "He got me in."

"Have you been in on many murder cases?"

"Quite a few. Why?"

"What sort of people do the murderers usually turn out to be?"

"Just like anybody else," he said promptly. "Murder is one crime that most anyone can commit. You have to be

smart to be a safecracker, and if you're going to be a sec-
ond-story man you've practically got to be an acrobat. But
any mug can pull off a murder. Why, I remember one case
where the killer turned out to be a school teacher. A quiet,
well-behaved guy that you'd never suspect. Looked like
you, as a matter of fact. Wore glasses, too. He killed his
wife with a ten-cent-store hatchet, cut her up, and burned
the pieces in the furnace. He was dumb enough to put the
ashes out in an ashcan, though." Anderson kept looking
at me steadily. "Say," he said suddenly, "that guy was a
dead ringer for you, all right. You didn't have a brother
or something? . . . What's so funny about that?" he asked
Henry, who was chortling with glee.

"Mr. Hale has a somewhat morbid sense of humor," I
said. "I'm afraid he's getting hysterical. He needs a little
hydrotherapy." I leaned over and pushed Henry's quivering shoulders. He fell into the brook with a loud splash.

CHAPTER XXIV
PARTY LINE

The afternoon dragged on, hot and oppressive. A few scattering drops of rain fell and the wind soughed through the trees as though a storm were coming. Anderson tried to tell us some stories of his experiences in other murder cases but we were a bad audience. Henry and I were nervous and jumpy and our uneasiness communicated itself to Joan and Helen, although they, of course, had no idea of our plans for the night.

After a dinner during which we all seemed to be at our grumpiest, Henry announced his intention of driving to Calverton. He told the girls that he wanted to look up some more alibis there. Anderson and I, as we had previously arranged, offered to accompany him and we drove off about seven o'clock after advising Emma to wait for us to take her back to the village even if we didn't return until late.

I drove fast, skittering around the dangerous curves on the North Brook road. As we passed the entrance to the Stanton tenant farm I slowed up almost involuntarily. It was still light, of course, and I could see the huge sycamore from which Howard Stanton's body had been hanged.

"I hope tonight finishes this affair," I said to Henry. "I've had enough. There's been too much excitement for my old nerves."

He grinned rather feebly. "You'd better brace up those old nerves for some final shocks," he said. "I've got my trusty automatic with me now. Wait till the fireworks start going."

"Have you taught this Boy Scout how to handle a gun without shooting his own thumb off?" I asked Anderson.

"Yeah, he's better now. He knows which end the bullets come out."

"He'll be a big help. Maybe you'd better let me have his gun."

"He won't need to do any shooting," Anderson said. "That's what I'm here for. I just let him have a gun to make him happy."

"Is he good?" I asked Henry.

"He's all right. He throws pennies in the air and clips 'em. He has medals, too."

"You must come out for the hunting season," I said to Anderson. "Maybe we could get enough rabbits to make a pie."

"I don't like to shoot rabbits," he said. "They're such cute little cusses. It makes me feel bad to kill 'em."

"But you don't mind shooting people?"

"Well," he said quizzically, "I haven't seen any rabbits yet that carried guns. When I shoot at a man it's usually because he has some idea about shooting at me first."

We turned into the main street of Calverton and stopped in front of the house where the local telephone exchange is installed. Anderson got out and went in to talk to the operator.

"Where's your gun?" I asked Henry.

"In the pocket of the door alongside you. Gosh, I wonder if I'll really have to use it?"

"If Anderson is as good as you say he is, it doesn't look as if you'll have the chance. Unless the murderer has a brigade with him, of course."

We sat in the car for a few minutes looking glumly at the quiet streets of the little town. Anderson finally came out of the telephone exchange.

"Okay! I got it all fixed," he said, getting into the car. "She promised to stay on duty all night if necessary and she's going to call us at Fammel's store."

"You'd better step on it," Henry said. "It's getting dark early tonight. I hope this rain holds off until it's all over."

I pushed Little Bertha along at a reckless speed. In the deep valley along the North Brook it was so dark under the trees that I had to turn the lights on. But it was still fairly light when we came out in the open on the last long hill leading down to Brookdale.

We left the car just outside the village and walked through the underbrush to the back of Joe Fammel's store.

"You two wait out here by the back door," Anderson whispered. "I'll get Fammel to open up and let us in."

We stood there silently in the swiftly growing darkness. Henry had slipped the big Colt automatic into his hip pocket as we left the car, and Anderson had his flashlight with him.

In a few minutes Joe Fammel came around the corner accompanied by Anderson. Joe was carrying a big brass key and he looked frightened. He greeted us in a low voice.

"Don't put any lights on," Anderson cautioned. "We may as well stay here in the back room until the phone rings. If it does ring," he added, looking at Henry.

We all sat down on the floor below the window level. Joe kept kerosene back there and the place smelled most unpleasantly of it.

We sat there in absolute silence for about fifteen minutes. Suddenly the phone rang.

Henry jumped to his feet.

"That ain't for me," Joe said. "My call is two short and one long. That's one long and two short. It's for Miss Harvey. She's likely to tie up the line for an hour if that's her niece from Calverton."

Henry looked desperate.

"Can't we get her off that wire?" he asked Anderson. "Tell her it's a police case."

"And tell everyone on this party line that we're lying in wait here? Don't be dumb," Anderson snapped.

The telephone continued to ring. Suddenly it stopped.

"Maybe I ought to listen in," Anderson said, and began to crawl on hands and knees toward the front of the store.

In a few minutes he returned.

"Is the niece's name Mabel?" he asked Joe.

Joe nodded.

"Well, it's the niece then all right, and from the way they're going, I'd say they can keep it up all night. It seems that Mabel's husband swore at his little wifie because she burned the steak. And he didn't like the coffee, either."

Henry groaned. "Do you suppose that operator will have sense enough to cut in on their call if anything happens?"

"I told her to do that very thing," Anderson said. "But no one can put in an outgoing call on this party line as long as they're talking."

"Damn Mabel. Maybe her husband will throttle her."

"He can't," Anderson said. "He went out of the house and slammed the door. That's what Mabel is particularly sore about."

Henry sighed.

It grew darker and darker in the little room behind Joe Fammel's store. Anderson had gone to listen in on the Harvey call several times. Mabel was evidently telling her aunt the whole story of her married life. It seemed that it had been all wrong ever since the honeymoon when they had gone to Atlantic City instead of Niagara Falls.

It was pitch-dark when Anderson came back with the good news that Mabel had finally hung up, determined to divorce her husband.

"She won't do it," Joe Fammel observed sagely. "I've heard all that before. She threatens to divorce him every week or so, but he's got a good job in the creamery, and

Mabel had a hell of a time landing him in the first place. She weighs over two hundred pounds and she ain't so young as she might be."

We sat in the darkness without talking for several minutes. The floor was getting awfully hard.

"Well, I guess you had a bum steer," Anderson said at last, evidently speaking to Henry. "It looks as if nothing was going to happen. You said that it would be right after dark."

"It's not so late yet," Henry said.

"It's ten minutes of nine," Anderson said, consulting the radium-faced dial of his wrist watch. "I'll wait ten more minutes."

The minutes crept by with dreadful slowness as I wriggled uncomfortably on the wooden floor.

"One minute to go," Anderson warned. "It looks like—"

And then the telephone rang! Two short and one long. Two short and. . . . Anderson rushed to the phone.

"Yeah. Okay, baby. Yeah. Mrs. Denner, huh?"

We gathered anxiously around the phone.

Anderson was listening to the operator. We could hear her excited voice but the words were too indistinct to make out.

"All right, and much thanks," he said at last and hung up. He turned around to face us.

"Mrs. Denner just called headquarters, Dr. Stanton has been attacked. On the lawn in front of the house. Right alongside the brook. Somebody tried to choke him and hit him over the head. She heard him yell. He's not dead. Unconscious though. Whoever it was got away. But she heard something splashing in the brook when she got there!"

"Well," I said impatiently, "let's get going. Dr. Stanton ought to know who it was that attacked him. When he comes to—"

"No," Henry burst out, "that's not the way to do it. We have a chance to catch the murderer red-handed now. We can question the doctor any time."

"I think we ought to go to the Stanton farm," Anderson said uneasily. "I should, anyway. They've put in a call for the police."

Henry was furious. "I'm handing you the chance to distinguish yourself in this case by getting the murderer in action. Are you going to be fool enough to pass it up? I need only ten minutes. Ten minutes, I tell you."

"All right," Anderson said reluctantly. "I'll stick around for ten minutes. But I've got to go up there then. What do you want me to do?"

"You stay here on the porch," Henry told Joe Fammel. "We'll yell if we need you. But don't budge off the porch meanwhile or you may get hurt. Come on," he said seizing Anderson's arm. "Let's go."

They hurried along the road leading to the west end of the village. I followed anxiously behind them. Henry stopped about a hundred feet beyond Fammel's store and just out of sight of it. The North Brook flows under a little bridge there.

"We can lie down alongside this stringpiece so we'll be out of sight in case he flashes a light on the bridge," Henry said. "Now, for the love of Mike, keep quiet and wait." He was pulling the big Colt automatic out of his pocket. Anderson slid his heavy police gun out of its holster, took his flashlight in his left hand, and obediently lay down on the edge of the road alongside the sheltering timber. Henry crawled into position at Anderson's feet and motioned to me to lie down also.

I did so, but I felt rather foolish, and I dreaded the thought that a car might come along while the three of us were stretched out there like drunken bums in a gutter.

The night was very still. I could hear the water of the brook gurgling gently underneath us and from time to time a distant whippoorwill sent out its call. Henry kept peering over the edge of the heavy beam.

I lay there absolutely motionless. I thought again of that night when I had found the body of Howard Stanton hanging over the brook in the darkness. I remembered what Whiskey Joe had said about a "beast splashing in the brook," and Mrs. Denner, too, only a few minutes ago had said. . . .

Henry was whispering excitedly. "I saw a flash of light. He must be coming now."

I heard Anderson getting himself ready for action. I peered cautiously over the big timber. The darkness was intense. The brook ran through a tangle of trees and underbrush that shut out even the dim glow of light from the cloudy night sky. Then I saw it—a momentary flash of light from a searchlight held close to the water by someone who was trying to find his way along the bottom of the brook. Brush grew close to the edge of the stream and one could get through at this point only by wading in the water, I knew that from trout fishing. The flash vanished almost instantly. A few seconds later it appeared again, this time a little closer.

"Down," Henry whispered in a barely audible voice, "keep down."

The flash of light had been less than a hundred feet away and it was coming toward us slowly but inexorably. I hugged the stringpiece closely. I heard the sound of splashing as though someone had stumbled in the water. There was a muffled exclamation and then, a different voice answered!

I stuck my head cautiously above the stringpiece. It was still pitch dark. I peered into the blackness. Suddenly a bright circle of light hit the water not fifteen feet away from us. I could see the vague outline of a body behind it. It went out. Now I could hear the feet of the murderer splashing in the brook.

I was aware of Anderson rising to his feet with his flashlight in his hand. He pressed the switch and the white beam shot through the darkness. Not six feet from me was the distorted figure of Edgar Harmon carried on the shoulders of his idiot son!

Harmon's eyes were wide-open and glaring and the
enormously dilated pupils stared unblinkingly into the
light. He shouted and I could see him struggling to get an
old army revolver out of a holster that was strapped to his
waist. The gun flashed in the light as he pulled it free, but
before he could fire there was a single deafening report
from beside me on the bridge. Harmon dropped his pistol.
His son shrieked wildly as his father's body toppled and
fell heavily into the water.

"Don't shoot him," I yelled.

"Okay," Anderson said tersely, watching the boy disap-
pear into the wilderness of brush. "Let's get his father out
of the water. I hit him in the hand."

Joe Fammel came running up.

"Hold this light," Anderson told him, thrusting the
flashlight into his hands. "Keep it pointed down on the
water so we can pull him out."

Anderson went around the end of the bridge and climbed
down. He splashed into the water and waded out to where
Harmon's body was lying face down in the shallows. He
turned it over. The pale face gleamed whitely in the rays
of the searchlight. There was a great gash on the side of
the forehead from which the blood was oozing sluggishly.

"He must have hit a rock when he fell," muttered
Anderson. "Too bad, but I had to do it. He was going to
shoot all right and he didn't care what at."

"It's probably just as well," Henry said. "He was completely insane—raving mad, and I don't think he had long
to live anyway."

Anderson picked up the limp figure. The clothing was
wet and cold, and the shattered hand dripped blood. We
laid the body down on the bridge where I examined it
in vain for any signs of life. Then Anderson, who had
stopped to retrieve the old Spanish-American War pistol,
rejoined us, and we carried Edgar Harmon across the road
to the dark, silent house that had been his home.

CHAPTER XXV
HENRY TELLS HIS STORY

We left Joe Fammel in charge and hurried back to our car. My foot hurt me but I kept on going. Anderson held his searchlight on the road, and as we turned the corner near Marigold's house, we saw two brilliant eyes shining in the darkness ahead of us. A Siamese cat scurried out of our way and crawled through the white picket fence that surrounds Marigold's property.

"Grimalkin is walking tonight," Henry said as we ran by. "I wonder if his master is in bed reading again. There isn't any light in the house."

I looked back at Marigold's house just in time to see a light jump on in one of the downstairs windows.

"Oh, yes there is," I said. "A light just went on."

He stopped for a moment to look.

"He's probably getting up to let his familiar in," he said, catching up to me.

Anderson was already in the car. He threw on the light switch and the headlights sent a glaring beam down the road toward us. I jumped in, started the engine, and turned around in one swoop. We dashed off toward the Stanton house. George Hathaway came out to meet us even before we had shut the engine off. There was a worried look on his homely face.

"He's still out," he said. "I hope he don't die."

We went inside. It seemed as though every kerosene lamp in the house had been lighted. There was an old single-barreled shotgun on the kitchen table.

The doctor was stretched out on the familiar horsehair sofa in the little parlor. Mrs. Denner was standing over him holding a bottle of smelling salts. Anderson threw the bright rays of his flashlight on the doctor's face as I bent over to examine him. He was breathing with great difficulty and I could see swollen red fingermarks on his throat. There was a contusion on the right side of his head. The skin had been broken and blood was matted in the iron-gray hair.

"I'm afraid there's nothing we can do," I said. "He'll be all right though, I should think. Have you called a doctor?"

"I called Dr. Adams," Mrs. Denner said, "but he's out on a delivery case. I kind of hated to call Dr. Sampson, seeing as how he was here last to look at poor Mr. Stanton's dead body. Do you suppose I ought to phone him?"

"You'd better," I said shortly.

She left the room and I turned to Henry.

"He's been deliberately hit on the head all right. He never could have got a blow like that in falling."

"I thought he'd be hit with a stone," Henry said coolly. "It was part of the technique. Harmon grabbed from behind. Probably let himself be pulled off his son's shoulders. Then he'd cling to his victim while Emmett helped with a rock."

"I suppose they'll pick up the boy somewhere," I said. "I don't like to think of his being at large."

"They'll get him all right. He hasn't got brains enough to get away by himself. I don't think he's dangerous, though. He obviously did everything under his father's direction. Even when he pushed the boulder down on me I realized that it was Harmon who had put him up to it."

"You're sure Emmett was alone when he did that boulder job?"

"Of course. His father couldn't do any traveling in the daylight. He told the boy just what to do. He obviously directed him when he visited your house and turned off the lights, too. And he doubtless wrote that nice little note for me with its symbolic pebble and string."

"That was a smart bit of work you did in spotting him," Anderson said admiringly.

"What made you suspect him?" I asked.

"Well," said Henry, "it was what is usually known in detective stories as psychological intuition. I realized that—"

A police siren sounded shrilly.

"Here they come," Henry said. "I might as well wait until they get here before I tell my little tale."

Anderson started suddenly. "Oh, nuts!" he groaned, "I left my motorcycle at your house. I'm going to catch hell for letting myself get separated from it."

Macready and his gang descended on us in approved movie fashion. There were six of them and they burst in carrying, among other artillery, two submachine guns.

The captain scowled when he saw me. "You here again?" he said. "Where's the body?"

"The body's still alive," Henry told him. "The doctor is, I mean. He's inside, in the parlor. We got the man who attacked him. Caught him in the act—almost."

"Where is he? Who was it?"

"He's dead. Anderson had to shoot," Henry said soberly. "It was Edgar Harmon."

"The cripple?" Macready seemed incredulous.

"Yes, the cripple. His son carried him. It was quite an ingenious trick."

"Must have been," the captain grunted. "But how about Dr. Stanton? How is he?"

"He's still unconscious, but I think he'll be all right," I said. "I was hoping Dr. Sampson would be with you."

"Dr. Stanton is still unconscious?" the captain said wonderingly. "Then, how did you know who the murderer was?"

"Ah, yes," Henry said. "How did I know who the murderer was? You may remember that I tried to tell you who he was one afternoon in Fammelton. You didn't want to listen then."

"You mean that stuff about 'psychological patterns'?" Macready snorted. "You've been reading too many books."

We all trooped into the parlor and stared solemnly at the doctor's motionless figure. He was breathing more normally and it looked to me as if he would soon regain consciousness.

Macready stomped out of the room and seized upon Anderson who had stayed in the kitchen looking like a lamb ready for slaughter.

"Now, what's this all about?" he growled. "Tell me the whole story. Start from the beginning and go slow. Come on, make it snappy."

"Yes, sir," Anderson said unhappily. "Mr. Hale saw me at the Morgan house this morning. Said he thought the murderer would go into action tonight. He had some kind of idea about how he—I mean the murderer—was going to use the brook to travel in so he wouldn't be seen."

"Uh? Say, you," the captain said, pointing to Henry, "you'd better tell this yourself. Maybe you can make some sense out of it. What's all this about traveling in the brook?"

Henry sat down on one of the kitchen chairs and calmly drew out a pack of cigarettes which he offered around. Everybody declined so he drew one out himself and lit it.

"I guess we'd better start at the beginning as you so very wisely suggested. Now to get back to the business of psychological patterns which I was telling you about several days ago when you so rudely interrupted me—"

"Skip all that," the captain said. "Get down to business, and tell us about the murder."

"I can't," Henry said firmly. "It all starts with psychological patterns. There weren't any useful material clues left in the Stanton murder—at least I couldn't find any by the time I got here. Your men had trampled all over everything. All I had to go on was the psychology of the murderer.

I must start with that. I'll try to put it in one-syllable words though."

"I don't care if you tell it in Chinese," Macready said, "so long as you get on with your story."

Henry smiled. "Yes, sir," he said meekly. "Now to get back to the subject—the Stanton killing called for a specific type of murderer. Howard Stanton, we know, was killed by strangulation, his head was beaten in by a stone, and then his dead body was hanged to a tree. Each of these things is not without significance. If you were going to kill a man in a lonely country place probably the simplest way to do it would be to shoot him. The shot wouldn't draw very much attention—certainly it didn't when we did a little shooting in the center of the village tonight. Or perhaps you might hit your victim over the head with a club of some sort.

"Shooting or clubbing are both reasonably efficient ways to kill but they lack one thing—clubbing less so than shooting, I admit—that throttling your victim gives. And that is the personal satisfaction that a killer must feel when he gets his hands around the throat of a hated enemy. There was no doubt in my mind that Stanton must have been hated by his slayer with a hatred that was venomous and almost inhuman. There would be, I felt sure, a motive for the killing that would be an extremely powerful one—one that would transcend such relatively trivial things as money or a personal difference of some petty origin. Howard Stanton's murderer, I was convinced, had good reason to hate him and he had been nursing his hatred for a long time.

"So we have a murderer, who, at great personal risk, resolves to kill Stanton with his bare hands. Then, curiously enough, we find that his victim was struck on the head with a stone, and—this is the curious part of it—he was struck with a fairly light blow. Now it hardly seemed reasonable to me that a man who was still in the emotional frenzy induced by feeling his enemy's life ooze out under his bare hands would tap the victim gently on the head when he had finished. I felt that it was more likely that he would pound his face to a jelly. Consequently I suspected the presence of a second person who went to the assistance of the murderer. I couldn't be sure, of course, but that is how I had the blow on the head figured out."

Henry paused for a moment, looking for a place to discard his cigarette. He was about to drop it on the floor when Mrs. Denner hurriedly handed him a saucer.

"Well, gentlemen," Henry continued, "it's perfectly true that there might have been several people who hated Howard Stanton enough to have killed him by strangulation. And any one of them, of course, might easily have had an accomplice. But now we come to the part where the murderer really gave himself away. You said at one time"—Henry nodded toward the captain—"that the killer signed his murders. Well, he did this one all right. Anybody might have strangled Stanton. Bill Morgan might very well have done so. He had ample cause, I think. But he wouldn't have stopped to get a rope from the field and go through the business of hanging Stanton's corpse. And not just stringing him up with a rope, mind you, but actually hanging him, tying a hangman's noose, and then letting the inert body drop so that the neck would be broken. That is something that could only have been done by"—Henry paused for a moment and drew out another cigarette—"by a madman," he finished quietly.

"Well," said Macready judiciously, "it *was* a sort of nutty thing to do. I always thought that. Any guy in his right senses would be making a getaway instead of playing around with a corpse."

"Exactly," said Henry, lighting his cigarette, and inhaling it deeply. "That's why I felt that Howard Stanton was killed by a person whose mind was deranged, by someone who had good cause to hate him terribly, and by a madman who could have an accomplice—and, after all, very few madmen could. A sane man isn't ordinarily likely to help a homicidal maniac. That's why Edgar Harmon and his idiot son were the only ones in this community who fitted into my psychological pattern. The hitch was, of course, that Harmon couldn't walk. But he could be carried by his son, and, as we have seen, they made a dangerous combination!"

"But you had no proof of any kind," Macready said pettishly.

"That's right," Henry agreed. "I had no proof. But I suspected what the motive was—and one day, when I noticed that Harmon's pupils didn't contract when exposed to a strong light, although they did when he looked at the paper he was reading, I knew that I had the reason for his action. He displayed the typical Argyll-Robertson pupil— the telltale symptom of—"

There was a scuffling sound in the bedroom, and Henry stopped short as the haggard face of Dr. Stanton appeared in the doorway. The doctor clung to the wall for support. Mrs. Denner ran to assist him.

"I heard what you were saying," he said in a faint voice. Mrs. Denner helped him to a chair. "I heard what you were saying," he repeated, "and I came in to tell you that you were right."

"Don't you want a bracer or something?" Macready asked gruffly.

The doctor waved him away impatiently. He looked straight at Henry and said: "Edgar Harmon, as you suspected from the Argyll-Robertson pupil, is a paretic—"

Henry stopped him. "Was, you should say," he told him. "Edgar Harmon is dead. He was killed when we tried to take him."

The doctor stared at Henry for a moment, then he continued: "Perhaps it is a good thing. He was on the verge of insanity, of course, and his insanity, as well as the imbecility of his son and his wife's suicide—the whole miserable tragedy of his life, in fact—was caused by my brother!"

"I was afraid so," Henry said softly. "It happened during the Spanish-American War, didn't it?"

The doctor nodded. "Howard got Hannon drunk one night when they were in Cuba. He was a green young country boy then, of course. Howard took him into the red-light district of one of the smaller towns there. . . ."

"I see," said Henry. "I thought it must have been something like that. No wonder he hated him so!"

"Edgar Harmon was a very rational person though," the doctor said. "A very fine person. He never blamed Howard—until his mind began to give way and the hatred he had suppressed for nearly forty years burned into his diseased brain."

"You knew all along that he had killed your brother?"

The doctor was silent for a moment. "I suspected it," he admitted finally. "I couldn't be sure."

"But you knew that he was a menace to the community? That he was insane and might kill again?"

"I should have had him committed to an asylum, I suppose."

"You might have prevented the necessity for a second murder if you had. And Mary Morgan would probably still be alive. It would have been better for everybody."

"I suppose so," the doctor said unhappily.

There was a slight pause. Henry looked around at the row of faces.

"Well," he said, "I guess we'd better get on to the second murder. The killing of Whiskey Joe, I mean. We know that Harmon couldn't have done that."

Macready looked at him questioningly.

"He couldn't have," Henry said. "The person who killed Whiskey Joe had a car. Certainly neither Harmon nor his son could drive an automobile. And besides, Mr. Whitby and I were in the same room with Edgar Harmon and his son at the time Whiskey Joe was killed."

CHAPTER XXVI
PARLOR TRICKS

"Well, I suppose you have the solution for the second murder all worked out for us?" Macready said in a tone that expressed many things.

"I may be able to cast some light on it," Henry said modestly.

"Perhaps it was Harmon's idiot son who did the killing."

Henry was impatient. "I've just been all through that. Don't you pay any attention to what I say? The presence of an automobile, the fact that we were in the room with him—"

"All right," the captain said hurriedly. "So he didn't do it. Now tell us who did."

"Have you got a quarter?" Henry asked.

"A quarter?"

"A quarter. A quarter of a dollar. Standard United States currency of any year or mint origin. Hasn't anybody got a quarter? I promise to return it intact. I need a few props to do my little act."

"I don't like parlor tricks even when they're good," the captain grumbled, but he handed Henry a quarter.

"You'll like this one," Henry said genially. "Now, I'll also need a stethoscope. Doctor, will you lend me your stethoscope? The small wooden one you carry with you."

The doctor struggled to pull the stethoscope out of his pocket.

Henry looked at the injured man with compassion.

"I think you do need a bracer," he said. "Mrs. Denner, why don't you take the doctor into his study and let him fix himself something to drink? I think he needs it."

The doctor looked strangely at Henry for a moment and then got waveringly to his feet.

Mrs. Denner led him from the room. Henry drummed on the table with his fingers for a moment. Then he fumbled in his pocket and drew out an envelope.

"Now, Captain Macready," he said, "I will tell you who killed Joseph Hartram. But first I'm going to tell you how I know."

"Okay," the captain said with a sigh. "But get on with it."

Henry leaned back in his chair. "This is my first bit of evidence," he said producing the scrap of burlap from the Eureka bag. "It is a piece of the cloth used by the killer of Whiskey Joe to bind his feet in so he would leave no identifiable footprints. I recovered it from the brook where the murderer waded to his car. I have been able to trace it by means which I will explain later, if necessary, to a shipment of special feed bags made last fall to Howard Stanton. It indicates, I should think, that the murderer had access to the barn on this property."

Macready stared curiously at the little scrap of burlap. "I've seen this already. You'll need better evidence."

Henry nodded. "We know, of course, that one of the tires on the car used by the person who killed Whiskey Joe had on it a V-shaped cut. Plaster casts of that mark were made. I felt certain that the person who did the killing would be clever enough to change his tires afterwards. Nevertheless I made a careful examination of all the cars in the neighborhood. I found no car carrying such a mark on any of its tires. But I did find something else of interest.

"An automobile owned by someone in this community has had all four of its tires removed recently. There are fresh scratches on the rim bolts, mud has been knocked from the rims, and the tires, which are not new tires, show indications of having been placed on the rims a very short time ago. All this proves nothing perhaps, but I do think it is significant that the spare tire, an unused shoe mounted on the rear of the car, has not been taken off the tire rack for a long time. The bolt locking it there, in fact, is rusted fast.

"Now it is my belief that the person who killed Whiskey Joe drove to a repair station in some distant town and had four second-hand tires placed on the rims of his car. He made the mistake of allowing his spare to stay on the tire rack."

"We could probably find the place that sold the tires," Macready said thoughtfully.

"Yes, I think perhaps you could. I hope it won't be necessary though, because I have other much more conclusive evidence. After all, it is conceivable that someone else might have used the car. I now wish to produce what I consider my most important evidence."

He opened the envelope and drew from it two photographic prints. He handed one of them to the captain. We crowded around to see it. It was the photograph of Whiskey Joe's body that Henry had taken the night we found him murdered in his bed. On the chest was a round black spot, and beside it was a hardly visible circle.

"The black spot is a quarter that I put there in order to establish the scale of the photograph. I'll show you what I mean."

He handed us the other print. It was an enlargement, thrown up many times, of the area surrounding the quarter. The coin was obviously a full-sized quarter. The dark circle next to it was rather larger than the coin.

"I have made this enlargement to the exact size of the original," he said. "And the size can be proved, of course, by placing an actual quarter over the print."

Henry laid the photograph on the table and placed Macready's quarter over its photographic facsimile. It covered it exactly.

"Now," said Henry, his voice rising, "what we are interested in is not the quarter, which shows nothing but the scale of the photograph, but the circle alongside it. That circle is practically the signature of the murderer, and I can prove beyond a reasonable doubt who left it there on Joseph Hartram's body!"

There was absolute silence for a moment, and then, from the front of the house, there came the shrill cry of a woman's voice, and Mrs. Denner came running toward us.

"He's killed himself!" she shrieked.

Henry drew a long breath.

"Well," he said, "that's better than going to the chair." He picked up the doctor's little stethoscope and dropped it over the circle on the photograph. It fitted neatly.

Dr. Stanton's body was slumped in a chair beside his brother's roll-top desk. There were fragments of a glass scattered on the floor around him, and his kit bag stood open on the desk.

"He was writing a prescription," Mrs. Denner said, sobbing. "He asked me to give it to Mr. Hale, and then he poured out something and drank it. He fell right over."

Henry stretched out his hand and Mrs. Denner gave him a folded slip of white paper. It was a prescription blank, but the doctor had written on it:

> *Mea culpa.* As you have probably suspected, I encouraged Edgar Harmon in his insane plot against my brother. For fifty years I have suffered as only a younger brother can. Howard not only managed to secure for himself our father's estate but also the woman I loved. And he drove her to her death. I should have killed him then. I am ashamed to say that one of the contributing factors in what I have done is now purely economic. Howard had lent me

money on my house as security and he had actually threatened to foreclose!

I knew I could use Edgar Harmon, who was already marked for death, as a destroying force against my brother. Unfortunately Joseph Hartram saw what no man was intended to see, and I had to act to protect myself as well as Harmon. I hope that his son will be taken care of. I have too much on my soul already.

The note was signed in full and dated. Macready immediately impounded it.

"Leave the body alone," he said. "I want the coroner to see it just as it is."

"Dr. Sampson's coming here," Mrs. Denner told him. "I telephoned him before."

"You'd better call the coroner, too," Macready said to Anderson. "He's going to earn his salary this year, all right."

We went out in the kitchen and sat down to await the arrival of Dr. Sampson and the coroner.

"You must have known the doctor was guilty ever since the night Whiskey Joe was killed," Macready said accusingly to Henry. "What were you waiting for?"

"I didn't know, I only suspected it," Henry said. "After all I couldn't be sure that it was his stethoscope that made the red circle on Whiskey Joe's chest. It wasn't until I saw Dr. Stanton using his stethoscope on Mr. Whitby the morning after he had been bitten by a snake that I was able to get anywhere. Every other physician around here uses a modern stethoscope which has a much smaller opening than this old wooden one. I went around checking up on them."

"Why didn't you tell us about it?"

"I couldn't establish the link between Harmon and the doctor. I knew who had committed the murders but I didn't have enough information about motives. When Mary Morgan killed herself I was sure that Harmon would make some overt move. I couldn't be sure just what he would do, so I had Anderson arrange with the local telephone operator to tip us off the minute anything happened. We waited at the phone in Fammel's store and when the call came through that the doctor had been attacked I was sure that it was Harmon who had done it. Especially since Mrs. Denner said she had heard someone in the brook. Anderson and I waited at the bridge near Harmon's house. I knew he would have to pass through there to get back home."

"I don't get that stuff about the brook," the captain said. "Why did he use the brook?"

"Harmon couldn't very well use the road," Henry told him patiently. "He was too conspicuous for that. And Emmett didn't have to wade all the way by any means. There's a fisherman's path along most of the brook and he doubtless took to it where he could. Down by the bridge the sides of the brook are so closely grown up with brush that the only way to get through is to walk in the water. The reason Harmon did his traveling at twilight is easy to understand. He wanted it dark enough so as not to be noticed but not so dark that his son couldn't see his way. He carried a flashlight, of course, to help out on the home stretch when it was really dark."

"What I want to know," Macready said to Henry, "is what started you off on the right track? What gave you the tip-off?"

"A book," Henry said with a faint grin. "A kid's book."

"Uh?"

"I don't know whether you read Aesop's *Fables* when you were young, Captain, but I had occasion to reread them recently. They're the only literary fare that my landlady has to offer, so I haven't had much choice. At any rate, Aesop tells a story about a blind man and a lame man who couldn't get anywhere by themselves, but when the blind man carried the lame man, they made a splendid team. It was a suggestion that offered food for thought since we had a similar situation right here in the village. And, of course, it fitted in beautifully with the psychological pattern—"

"Never mind that," the captain said hurriedly. "I admit you got the jump on us in this case, but all you did was use plain horse sense. You don't have to give it fancy names."

"Horse sense is a good general term for psychological intuition, Captain," Henry said. "It's all right with me."

"How is it nobody else saw the mark of the doctor's stethoscope on Whiskey Joe's chest?" Macready asked.

"Well, such a mark would last only a few minutes. It was nearly gone by the time I finished photographing it."

"Why do you suppose he used the stethoscope at all?"

"It's my guess that the doctor tried to kill Whiskey Joe by strangling in order to make it look as though the murder had been committed by the same person who killed Howard Stanton. It isn't very pleasant to choke an unconscious person to death, you know. In order to make sure that Joe was dead he probably listened for any heart action with the stethoscope. He must have pressed down rather hard with the instrument. He wanted to make sure. That pressure left the circular mark. When he realized that Joe wasn't dead he took a heavy stone from the pile outside the door, smashed it down on Joe's head, and then put the rope around his neck to complete the picture. I always thought it was highly significant that the murderer of Whiskey Joe had not brought a rope, but had used one he found in the shack. It showed that he had not thought the murder out very carefully beforehand."

"Sounds okay," the captain grunted. "And then he had the tires on his car changed?"

"Yes, and he was smart enough to get used tires to replace them with but he slipped up on the spare."

"I always said a murderer will miss some little thing that gives him away," Macready said sententiously.

Henry discreetly said nothing.

"How do you suppose the doctor got word of what Whiskey Joe had been saying in town that day?" I asked.

Henry looked at me and grinned. "I'm afraid we performed that little service for him."

"How do you figure that out?"

"Well, we told Harmon about it. Then when we went home to get our dinner I imagine that Harmon sent a note with Emmett to the doctor telling him that Joe was likely to spill the beans, and that something had to be done about it in a hurry. It was still daylight so Harmon couldn't do it."

"Do you think Joe really saw anything?"

"It's my guess that he may have seen one man being carried by another. That would be enough to implicate Harmon. It really doesn't matter, though, whether Joe saw anything or not. Harmon and the doctor thought he did and that was enough to make them have to put him out of the way."

"But how was the doctor able to plan the killing of his brother so it would take place while he was away in Cleveland?" I asked Henry.

"I'm afraid we'll never be able to learn the exact truth about that now," Henry said. "However, one way that he could have done it would have been to plant in Harmon's mind, just before he left town, the idea of being carried by his son."

"And then—?"

"Well, once Harmon had the idea given him he would probably want to put it into action as soon as possible. He must have known that he hadn't much longer to live as a free man outside an insane asylum. We know that Mrs. Denner had told her cousin over the party line that Stanton was going to work late in the fields that night. Anybody might have listened in. I imagine that it was probably Miss Harvey who innocently blabbed to Harmon when she came to prepare his dinner."

"Well," said Macready finally, "it all sounds very nice when you tell it, but I still think you might have had a tough time making out a case in court."

Henry nodded. "Perhaps. That's why I gave the doctor the chance to do what he did," he said gravely.

Dr. Sampson and the coroner finally came and did what their official duties called for. I was eager to get back to the house. I knew the girls would be worried.

The captain and his men picked up their artillery and climbed into the police car. Anderson shifted around uneasily.

The engine of the big police car started with a roar. Macready stuck his head out.

"Hey, you," he called to Anderson. "Where's your motorcycle?"

"I left it at Mr. Whitby's house," he said in a very small voice.

"A fine motorcycle cop you are," the captain growled. "Do you know what Regulation 27a of the Police Manual says?"

"Yes, sir," Anderson said meekly. "'Don't abandon motorcycle when on duty.'"

"Well then, walk," the captain shouted. "Get going."

"We could take him back with us," Henry volunteered.

"Like hell you will," the captain said. "He'll walk. And I'm going to make sure he'll walk. You two drive on ahead."

We got into our car. Anderson looked at us unhappily. "Okay. Go ahead," the captain yelled to us. "We'll follow you out."

We turned into the driveway.

"I'm glad I'm not a cop," Henry said.

"So far as I can see you're just a plain, ordinary cotton converter now," I told him. "You'll be back doing thread counts and other such exciting things before you know it."

"Don't remind me," Henry groaned. "I hate the very thought of it."

We drove along in silence for a few moments. Big juicy raindrops began to spatter on the windshield.

"Poor Anderson!" Henry said. "That was a filthy trick."

"We can have some hot coffee ready for him," I suggested. "He's rather partial to coffee. It's probably forbidden in the Police Manual, but maybe he can get away with one cup."

Henry slumped down in his seat and looked at the rain that splashed against the windows.

"What are you going to do with the rest of your vacation?" I asked idly.

"Oh, I'll stick around here, I guess. It's nice country. I've been thinking I might look around for a farm."

"A farm? What would a bachelor like you want with a farm?"

"Well, you never can tell," he said with a grin. "Every day I grow older. I've been thinking that perhaps I ought to settle down. Get married—"

"—have babies, raise cows and chickens," I snorted. "You're a damn fool. You don't know when you're well off."

"I'm tired of being well off," Henry sighed. "And besides, it's so lonesome."

"You won't be able to buy any more expensive cameras if you get married. You won't have a moment of your own. You won't—"

"I know. I've thought all about it."

"And anyway, what makes you think that Helen would marry you? She's a nice girl."

"Nothing. Nothing at all," he said meekly. "It's just wishful thinking."

"Well," I said magnanimously, "I'll give you a clue. I know women. I ought to, I'm married to one. I can always tell how they'll act because they all act alike. Now when we get back to the house, Joan is going to give me hell for staying out so late. She won't be at all concerned as to whether I've been in danger or not. After all, I might have been killed tonight but she won't think about that. She'll just be sore because I'm late. That's because we're married. But Helen, if she is really in love with you, is going to be terribly worried. They may have heard the shot Anderson fired. They certainly must know that something has happened. You watch Helen and see how she acts."

We were rapidly approaching the house. The headlight beam showed two small figures and a dog standing on the porch.

"Remember what I told you now," I said. "You can depend on it. I understand women."

"Yes, Father," Henry murmured, "I'm all agog." He was out of the car before I came to a full stop.

Joan ran out in the rain and jumped on the running board.

"Are you hurt?" she asked anxiously. "I was so worried. We heard a shot—"

I looked at her in surprise. "No, I'm not hurt," I said peevishly. "Why this sudden solicitude?"

"I was terribly worried about you," she said, kissing me. "Tell me what happened."

From somewhere in the darkness surrounding the car came the sounds of wrangling voices.

"You might have gotten back sooner," I heard Helen saying. "You know how—"

There was a smothered squeal.

"Don't look now," Joan whispered in great excitement, "but I think he's kissing her."

ABOUT THE AUTHOR

Peter Storme was the pseudonym for Philip Van Doren Stern (1900-1984), better known as an editor, anthologist, and respected historian-author (particularly about the Civil War). He was a proud alumnus of Rutgers University (being the first in his family to attend college). He is best known as the author of the short story, "The Greatest Gift," which was later filmed as *It's a Wonderful Life* (1946).

COACHWHIP PUBLICATIONS
COACHWHIPBOOKS.COM

THE
RUMBLE
MURDERS

Henry Ware Eliot, Jr.

COACHWHIP PUBLICATIONS
CoachwhipBooks.com

DEAD
WEIGHT
ADDISON
SIMMONS

COACHWHIP PUBLICATIONS
CoachwhipBooks.com

DRESSED
TO KILL

Emma Lou Fetta

COACHWHIP PUBLICATIONS
CoachwhipBooks.com

THE
BEACON HILL
MURDERS

∞

THE
BACK BAY
MURDERS

THE ROGER SCARLETT MYSTERIES
VOL. 1

COACHWHIP PUBLICATIONS
CoachwhipBooks.com

NOW I LAY ME
DOWN TO DIE

ELIZABETH TEBBETTS-TAYLOR

COACHWHIP PUBLICATIONS
COACHWHIPBOOKS.COM

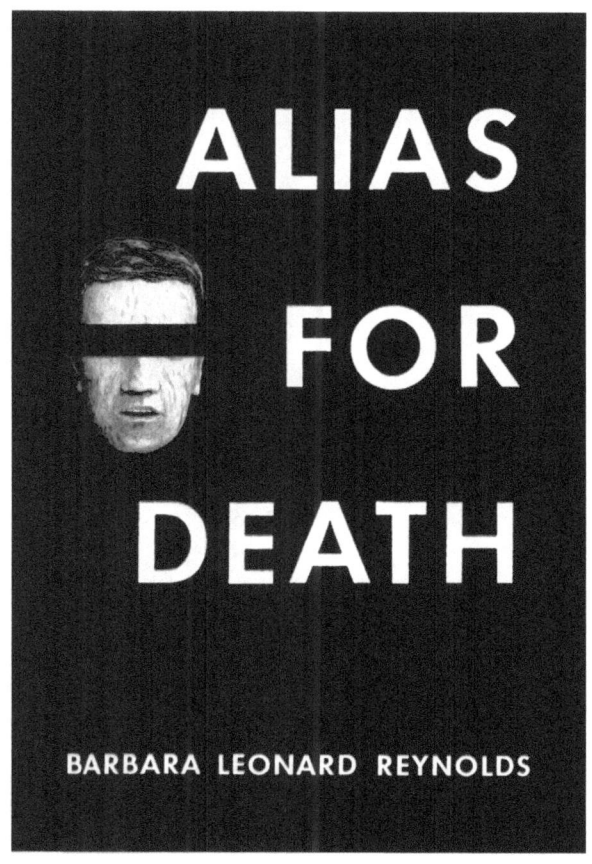

ALIAS

FOR

DEATH

BARBARA LEONARD REYNOLDS

COACHWHIP PUBLICATIONS
CoachwhipBooks.com

VIRGINIA RATH

DEATH AT
DAYTON'S FOLLY

COACHWHIP PUBLICATIONS
CoachwhipBooks.com

SAMUEL ROGERS

YOU'LL BE
SORRY!

YOU LEAVE
ME COLD!